A dark sedan zoomed by and entered the street side of the parking lot. A window came down. A gun came out.

Hunter saw the gun, glanced at the woman and then did what he had to do. He ran straight for Chloe and tackled her to the ground.

While silenced bullets spewed all around them.

Chloe tried to find air, tried to see over the brawny shoulder that shielded her face. "Let me up," she said, struggling.

"Stay still!"

He held her there but shifted, still covering her. She heard a motor revving and tires screeching. The car sped away, dirt and rocks flying in its wake. People came out of the restaurant, shouting and talking, pointing to where Hunter and Chloe lay. She'd barely heard the zing from the silencer but the people inside must have seen him diving over her.

"Are they gone?"

He lifted up to stare down at her, his breath warm on her neck. His eyes were a smoky gray that washed her in a questioning darkness. "I think so."

With over seventy books published and millions in print, **Lenora Worth** writes award-winning romance and romantic suspense. Three of her books finaled in the ACFW Carol Awards, and her Love Inspired Suspense novel *Body of Evidence* became a *New York Times* bestseller. Her novella in *Mistletoe Kisses* made her a *USA TODAY* bestselling author. Lenora goes on adventures with her retired husband, Don, and enjoys reading, baking and shopping...especially shoe shopping.

Books by Lenora Worth

Love Inspired Suspense

Men of Millbrook Lake

Her Holiday Protector
Lakeside Peril

Rookie K-9 Unit

Truth and Consequences

Capitol K-9 Unit

Proof of Innocence

Texas K-9 Unit

Lone Star Protector

Fatal Image
Secret Agent Minister
Deadly Texas Rose
A Face in the Shadows
Heart of the Night
Code of Honor
Risky Reunion
Assignment: Bodyguard
The Soldier's Mission
Body of Evidence

Visit the Author Profile page at Harlequin.com for more titles.

LAKESIDE PERIL

LENORA WORTH

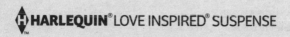

HARLEQUIN® LOVE INSPIRED® SUSPENSE

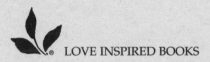

® LOVE INSPIRED BOOKS

ISBN-13: 978-0-373-67781-8

Lakeside Peril

Copyright © 2016 by Lenora H. Nazworth

www.Harlequin.com

Printed in U.S.A.

Many sorrows shall be to the wicked;
but he who trusts in the Lord, mercy shall surround him.
–Psalms 32:10

To Bennie Riggs and the former Hog Wash Bar and Grill in Oklahoma City.

Many thanks to Glen and Tina Hughes for answering my questions about Oklahoma and oil! This one goes out to the men and women who work on the oil patches all over the world. I appreciate your hard work!

ONE

Someone was watching him.

He could feel the hair on the back of his neck rising while the purr of his pulse vibrated an all-too-familiar warning.

He never could relax, not really. Not even at a biker dive in the Florida Panhandle where he was trying to mind his own business.

Hunter Lawson took a sip of the club soda dripping with condensation and slowly lifted out of the chair where he sat on the deck of the Hog Wash Rib Joint.

A woman stood outside the open barn doors leading from the interior of the rickety restaurant that mostly accommodated bikers needing to wash their rides, eat some good food and get into a fight every now and then.

She was definitely not a biker chick.

But she stared at him with a determination that meant business. Harmless but lethal, all the same.

Hunter observed people. Doing so was his nature. So he took his time accessing *this* woman standing in *this* place. Didn't match up.

She was serious and svelte. Sleek in a country girl kind of way in her jeans and tan leather jacket. Her boots looked hand-tooled. Her eyes shone a deep golden-brown and her hair—the afternoon sun loved her hair. It was a russet gold that surrounded her face like an intricate frame. The look in her eyes shouted *trouble.*

Being a private investigator brought him in contact with a lot of interesting people. But this one was different. His gut burned with a hot warning.

"What?" Hunter asked, his hands out.

"I…I need a word with you, Mr. Lawson."

"Okay." Hunter motioned to his favorite table on the deck over the Millbrook River. "Step into my office."

Her expensive-looking boots clicked toward him and in the next instant a dark sedan zoomed by and entered the street side of the parking lot. A window came down. A gun came out.

Hunter saw the gun, glanced at the woman and then did what he had to do. He ran straight for her and tackled her to the ground.

While silenced bullets spewed all around them

Chloe tried to find air, tried to see over the brawny shoulder that shielded her face. "Let me up," she said, struggling.

"Stay still!"

He held her there but shifted, still covering her. She heard a motor revving and tires screeching. The car sped away, dirt and rocks flying in its wake. People came out of the restaurant, shouting and talking, pointing to where Hunter and Chloe lay. She'd barely heard the zing from the silencer, but the people inside must have seen him diving over her.

"Are they gone?"

He lifted himself up to stare down at her, his breath warm on her neck. His eyes a smoky gray that washed her in a questioning darkness. "I think so."

He sat up and held out his hand to help her do the same. "You okay?"

Chloe wasn't sure how to answer that. Now that she'd found Hunter Lawson, a slow panic began to set in. What if he recognized her? What if he didn't even remember her? What if he told her to get lost? And how could she explain to him that someone was trying to kill her?

Taking her quiet for shock, he snapped his fingers in front of her eyes. "Hey, stay with me. Talk to me."

"I'm fine," she said, wishing she'd stayed in Oklahoma. Her friend Bridget Winston had tried to warn her that this was a bad idea. "Just a few scrapes and bruises."

And the imprint of him becoming a human shield still on her heart. He was big and strong and smelled as fresh and earthy as the fall air around them. He looked every bit as mysterious and unapproachable as people had tried to tell her. Dark, inky hair hovered over his collar in choppy, rebellious curls. Tanned, muscular arms and jean-clad legs. Battered cowboy boots. Dark aviator shades that he'd lost somewhere when he'd dived for her. And a concealed weapon tucked against the waist of his jeans.

Chloe had heard rumors regarding this man, but none of them quite lived up to seeing him in the flesh. She rubbed her sweaty palms against her jeans, her heart going into overdrive with each breath she took. Could she convince him to help her?

Please, Lord, let him listen to me.

He stood and helped her up. "Care to explain?"

"In private, yes," she replied.

People stood around everywhere, some with drinks in their hands. Leather moto jackets and tattoos, beat-up boots and graffiti T-shirts. Women clinging to their men, their gazes moving over her with cool curiosity while their attitudes told her to back off.

"Hunter, you all right, man?"

Hunter nodded to the bartender she'd spoken with earlier. He'd warned her, too. Explained t her that Hunter wasn't a talker. He only came here to sit out on the deck and watch the river roll by.

Well, her arrival had certainly changed all that.

Hunter glanced at her and then turned back to the bartender. "Yeah. Just someone trying to use me for target practice." He shrugged. "What else is new?"

"Do I need to call the police?" the burly man asked, his disapproving eyes on Chloe. He gave her a look that blamed her for all this action. And he was right.

"I'll take care of it," Hunter replied. Then he turned to Chloe and gave her his own harsh glare. "Just as soon as this nice lady explains to me why someone's shooting at her."

Reassuring herself that he wouldn't remember her because they'd never even met, Chloe swallowed back her trepidations and tried to find her footing. She wasn't giving up now. Not after making the agonizing decision to come across the country to find him. That shooter was proof of what she already knew.

"Can we go somewhere else and talk in private?" she asked.

He glanced at the crowd. The spectators didn't seem fazed by gunshots. They moved as one back into the restaurant, laughing and talking. "That depends on what we need to talk about."

"I want to hire you," she said, blurting it out because she was afraid the shooter would return. Or that Hunter would tell her to get lost.

He guided her to another table that was hidden from the street by a big weathered fence. "Sit here." Then he walked to the street side of the deck and looked both ways. Satisfied for now, he turned and stalked back to her. "Let's start with your name."

Chloe's heart rate increased. "Chloe Conrad."

His expression went from interested to intense, rage boiling up in his eyes. "What did you say?"

"Chloe. My name is Chloe."

"I heard that part," Hunter replied, standing. Would he leave her here? "Tell me your last name again."

She gave him a look of resolve. Followed by a look of disappointment. "Conrad," she said. "Yes, as in Conrad Oil. But I hope that won't be a problem."

His frown darkened, a vein throbbed along his jawline. "Conrad Oil. You'd better believe that's a problem. Sorry, lady, I'm not for hire."

Then he dropped a ten by his forgotten drink on the other table and stalked out to his waiting bike.

Chloe couldn't believe he'd just up and walked away without letting her explain. Marching ou to the parking lot, she caught up with him before he cranked the big black motorcycle. "Hey!"

He didn't move. Just stood there with his back to her, his hands on his hips, his head down.

Chloe swallowed and forged on. "It's about my sister, Laura. Somebody murdered her. And I'm pretty sure they're after me now."

Hunter stared down at Chloe Conrad, every vein in his body running hot with the sure knowledge that he needed to get on his bike, drive away and never look back.

But he couldn't do that. He had to understand why she'd come here all the way from Oklahoma to find him of all people. Since they'd just been shot at, he could only assume she was telling the truth. "What makes you think your sister was murdered?"

Her eyes became burnished with relief, but her expression filled with caution. "A small-engine plane she was piloting went down a few months ago. The authorities ruled it as pilot error, but Laura was an experienced pilot. I know something isn't right, but no one will believe me."

Her words echoed over Hunter and he remembered the sensation of thinking the same thing when his older sister had died in a car crash over three years ago. Something had not been right about the accident. No one had believed him, either.

At least no one from the Conrad family had believed him.

But he'd proven them all wrong.

"I can't help you," he said, the agony of the past hitting him in the gut.

"No," she said, grabbing his arm to keep him from trying to leave again. "Do not walk away from me. I hired a pilot to fly me down here even though I was afraid to get on a plane after what happened to my sister. I've been careful and I did my research. You're supposed to be the best at what you do and I know you're licensed in both Florida and Oklahoma, but if you treat all your clients the way you're treating me, you must have a lot of time to sit around staring at the water. Why won't you listen to me?"

He heard *that*. Surprised by the bit of fire that had just exploded inside this pretty package, Hunter glanced down at her soft, warm hand holding on to his wrist with a tight grip. But he still wasn't convinced that he should be the one to help her. "Those people will come back. You need to get out of here."

"I can't leave now," she said, her voice quiet, defeated. "If I get back in my rental car, they'll find me and kill me and then there won't be any justice for Laura. You might hate my father and my stepbrother, but Laura deserves more. A lot more."

Hunter closed his eyes, willing her to go away. But he couldn't send her out there to be slaughtered. When he heard a car turning into the drive, he glanced up and saw the same dark sedan. They were back.

He grabbed her and lifted her toward the bike. "Get on," he said, swinging his leg over the seat. Seeing the panic and fear in her eyes, he reached out for her. "Now!"

She stared at the car for a split second and then hopped on the motorcycle.

"Hold on," he said over his shoulder.

She wrapped her slender arms around his stomach, causing him to experience a strange, heavy discomfort followed by an acute awareness.

The dark car stopped, idling, the driver watching.

Hunter cranked the bike and took off behind the building and cut through on a side street. He had only minutes before the sedan would find them. So he zigzagged through the back streets and zoomed up and down alleys and driveways before he finally headed out to the one spot where he thought they'd be safe for a while.

He took her to the camp house.

TWO

Hunter didn't want to talk about anything that had to do with the Conrads, but he was deep into this now. He parked the bike up underneath the fat pilings that held the house sturdy and high off the ground and protected it during storms. Out over the water, a golden sky shimmered against the waves like a lace curtain. The sun was setting off to the west, but it cast out muted rays that turned the horizon into a kaleidoscope of color.

"We should be okay here for a while," he said as he helped Chloe off the motorcycle. She felt light in his arms, but the darkness in her eyes told of her exhaustion. "This place is secluded and off the beaten path."

Hunter knew he needed to help her. It was that simple.

But oh, so complicated. It went against every cell in his body to help anyone connected to the powerful Conrad family. This would be a betrayal of his sister's memory.

"Where are we?" she asked, glancing around at the fishing gear, four-wheelers and boats stored underneath the broad, square wooden house. She tossed her hair away and straightened her heavy leather jacket.

"We call it AWOL," he said. "It's a man cave I own with three of my friends. We hang out here on weekends and fish and…try not to talk much."

That won him a quiet smile.

"I see the water," she said, looking out past the palm trees and dense tropical foliage. "It's beautiful."

"It's the big bay," he explained. Hunter liked the openness of the water. He could breathe here. Most days.

He liked Florida. Funny how he'd just realized that.

"How did you wind up here?" she asked, probably to stall the inevitable questions he needed to ask her.

But he answered her, needing the time to gauge her and study her. Maybe get a feel for who she really was.

"Friends," he said.

He'd come down here a couple of years ago to visit Blain Kent after returning from one last tour of duty. Blain now worked for the Millbrook Police Department as a detective. They'd met in Oklahoma at a place similar to the Hog

Wash when Blain was passing through years ago. Almost got in a fight over a pretty woman, but when she'd told off both of them, they laughed and spent the rest of the night playing darts and talking shop, since they were both headed for deployment.

"A lifetime ago," he said, shaking his head.

He'd tried to put Oklahoma behind him.

Now it was staring him in the face with a pretty smile and sad eyes the same color as the sunset.

Blain was a former marine and this summer he'd married Rikki Alvanetti. Hunter had wound up in Special Forces. He still didn't like to talk about what he'd been through, so nobody bothered him about it. And he wasn't planning on going the way of his three buddies. Unlike Blain and their friends Rory Sanderson and Alec Caldwell, Hunter had no intention of settling down. Marriage and a family were not in his future.

He was a loner. Always had been.

He remembered how Alec, Blain and even Preacher had each brought a woman here. Now Alec and Blain were married and Preacher was next. Hunter had promised that would never happen to him.

But here he stood with a woman he didn't want to help, a woman who represented a big hurt in his lousy life. He would not take her inside this house. And yet he had to keep her out of sight.

She didn't ask any questions after he'd given her the lowdown, telling her only what he wanted her to know.

Motioning to a planked picnic table, he walked her over to the wooden Adirondack chairs the guys had built last summer. The table and chairs were hidden behind a thick row of bamboo stalks, but it gave him a good view of the road and the shell-covered lane leading up to the house. They could use the table as cover if they had to. He hoped it wouldn't come to that.

Satisfied with their surroundings, he stared at Chloe. "I need you to level with me."

"I told you, I need a private investigator," she said, stepping near before she sat down, her brown boots tight against her jeans, her perfume more exotic than the lilies Preacher had planted down by the shore. "And I'm willing to pay whatever price you name."

She smelled of money. Her family had a lot of it. He needed money, but he wondered what taking on her case would cost *him*. He didn't want any Conrad blood money.

She must have sensed his dilemma. "You saw those men. They won't stop until I'm dead."

"I kind of got that part after the fun we had back at the Hog Wash," he said. "You need to tell me everything, starting with why you came all this way *for me* when there's plenty of PIs in Oklahoma."

She looked out at the water glistening in a rich yellow-orange beneath the bronze sky, a second's worth of hesitation holding her still. "Because I heard that you lived here now and that you're licensed in both Oklahoma and Florida." Glancing over at him, she added, "I also heard you were the best."

"Who told you about me?"

Another evasive silence. "What does it matter? I'm here now. I thought I'd covered my tracks, but they followed me. I need someone I can trust."

He let out a sigh. "Be honest. I like honesty."

Her beautiful, defiant gaze hit him square in the face. "So do I. And that's why I'm here." She hesitated one more time before she sent him a worried stare and then plunged ahead. "Gerald Howard said you'd done some work for him."

Hunter grabbed the hair falling over his forehead and grunted. How had this nice October day gone from bad to worse in the span of a few minutes?

"I don't like Gerald Howard," he said, irrational feelings closing in on him from all sides. "He's a slick lawyer with his own agenda and he's your father's right-hand man. I parted ways with

Howard a long time ago. I don't get him recommending me for anything."

"I know you don't like Mr. Howard," she retorted, her words rushing together as swiftly as the bay's choppy current. "But he respects you and he says you deliver on the job."

"Yeah, I do my job," Hunter replied. Ignoring the irritating sensations she'd dredged up, he added, "Even when I don't like my clients."

"You don't have to like me," she retorted. "You just need to believe me when I say they are all involved."

"Who are *they*?" Hunter asked, figuring that was a loaded question. "Who *doesn't* believe you?"

"The sheriff in Conrad Corner, for starters." She glanced out at the water, a dark sadness that Hunter recognized coloring her eyes. "And just about everyone else there, too. Possibly including my father."

Conrad Corner, Oklahoma. Hunter didn't want to think about that dingy little town thirty miles west of Oklahoma City. He'd been running from that place since he'd returned stateside.

But he did believe one thing Chloe Conrad had said.

The sheriff in Conrad Corner was corrupt, so if the sheriff had refused to help her, there had to be a reason. And not a good one. Her father owned as many people as he did acreage.

"Keep talking," he said.

She had just become his client.

Chloe let out a breath she hadn't realized she'd been holding, tears of relief burning through her eyes. No one, not even her distraught family, wanted to delve into what might have happened on that deserted airstrip this past spring. But she'd found some details that made her believe finding Hunter Lawson was her only hope. Now she had to convince him to help without sharing all those details with him. Yet.

Knowing Hunter might actually believe her helped her to go on. "Over the last few months I've gone from mourning my sister's plane crash and death to promising myself to find out who killed Laura. Because besides knowing that Laura was an expert pilot, I found something else that disturbed me."

He drummed his fingers on the weathered table. "What?"

"Her apartment had been ransacked. Everything had been tossed around and knocked over. It happened a few days after her funeral."

"Did you report it?"

"Yes, but…nothing of value was missing. I don't think they found what they were looking for, since I'd already taken out a box of personal papers and files earlier in the week."

"So what happened after that?"

"I went through the files and papers I found at her apartment when I went to clean it out a day or so after the crash. My mother asked me to do it." She tugged at her jacket, took another breath. The anguish of going into that apartment tormented Chloe even now. "My sister was a social reporter. She did human interest stories for a humanitarian website and worked as a beat reporter at the *Conrad Chronicle*. She wasn't into hard news. Laura had such a good heart she always looked for the best in people."

"What did you find in the files?" Hunter asked, his tone quiet but his eyes cutting like gunmetal.

He wanted to be done with her. Discomfort and impatience radiated all around him like a mantle. Chloe decided now wasn't the right time to give him all the details. She had to gain his trust bit by bit.

"Some reports and notes regarding several parcels of land near Conrad. Land that my family secretly owns."

"Your family owns half of Oklahoma."

"But this is land that my father somehow bought up in bits. I think he's been quietly sitting on it for years. It looks as if someone bought it up under another name, even though the sales are public record. I couldn't understand why Laura would be interested in that until I studied these reports."

"What did the reports say?"

"From what I could gather, the land has been in a holding pattern with a company called Wind Drift Pass. Laura's notes indicated it was some sort of shell company. No one knows that Conrad Oil is involved with the transactions. But I think Laura found out something regarding this land, something that caused her death. She'd made notes indicating that Conrad Oil owned the land. I believe she was gathering information to confront someone. Or expose someone."

He sat back in his chair. "Big corporations use shell companies a lot to avoid paying taxes."

"Yes, but why would Conrad Oil use one for land that hasn't been developed yet? What are they trying to hide?"

"Why don't you ask your father that question?"

She sat silent for only a second, but Hunter's eyes turned a deep gray. So he answered the question for her. "Because you don't trust him."

Chloe hated to admit it, but it was the truth. And Hunter had asked for the truth. She gave him as much of it as she felt necessary for now. "I don't trust anyone."

He nodded. "Ah, so that explains it."

"What do you mean?" she asked. Had he already figured it all out?

He leaned up in his chair, his gaze pinning her. "Why you came to me."

THREE

Chloe slid around so she could face the water, sweat beading on her upper lip in spite of the cool air. This was a peaceful, secluded spot, but she felt anything but peaceful.

"I told you—"

"You know I hate your father, right?" Hunter asked, his hands gripping the wide arms of his chair. "So...you can't trust him, but you think maybe I'd be the perfect person to help you bring him down? Maybe because you think I need to seek revenge or retribution against your family? So you'll use me to handle the unpleasant tasks the same way your father uses people? Is that it? Am I right so far?"

He made it sound so sordid she wanted to bolt right out of here. But where would she go?

"That's not my reason for finding you," she said, fatigue warring with hope, regret merging with resentment. "I thought maybe if we worked together on this and if I could find out who did this to Laura, you might finally forgive my step-brother for what he did."

Anger clouded his eyes. "I doubt that's gonna work, since getting justice for you will not absolve anyone—not even me. Besides, I don't have to forgive Tray Conrad. He's dead now and I'm thinking he's *not* in a better place."

"But—"

"But hiring me is one thing. Trying to redeem Tray is another. We do this my way and that means we aren't going to speak of that lousy piece of humanity again, understand? And it also means I'm not anybody's whipping boy or killer-for-hire."

He stared out at the water for a moment and then gave her a look full of defiance. "I'll help you find the truth about your sister's death, but this doesn't have anything to do with my feelings toward your family. Nothing will ever make me change my mind on that. Understand?"

She nodded again and stared at her boots. "I'm sorry, Hunter. For what he did to your sister."

Hunter's brooding expression turned black with anger. "Save it and get on with things."

She told him more about the files she'd found, but she was still afraid to divulge everything. "I separated the files and kept some on my laptop and then hid part of them in a safe spot."

"Nowhere is safe if someone is after damaging information."

"I also took pictures of the papers and contracts that show the land sale. My father's signature is nowhere on *those* papers, but somehow Laura found out he's behind those buyouts."

"He probably had someone strong-arm the landowners. You know how he lets other people do his dirty work."

Hunter's disgusted tone was undeniable. He'd never forgive Wayne Conrad for trying to cover up what her stepbrother, Tray, had done. Why *had* she come here?

She stood, needing to be away from him. "This was a bad idea. If you'll take me back to the Millbrook Inn, I'll call a cab and get a flight home."

Hunter stood, too, and blocked her way, his broad chest shadowing the last of the sunset's show-off rays. "Not gonna happen."

"You said you hate my father."

"I do. But if I let you go back and something happens to you, I'll have to live with that, too."

"I don't want you to live with any more grief," she said, hoping he'd see the sincerity in her eyes. "I came to you because you know Oklahoma. You grew up there. You know the oil fields and you know how things work."

And because her sister had written his name with a question mark beside it in her notes. There were some other interesting revelations in her sister's papers, but Chloe figured she'd have to dole out those details one at a time with this man. Had Laura planned on finding him?

"Yeah, I know it all," he said in a taut whisper. "I watched my parents scrape and grovel just to keep a roof over our heads. My daddy worked himself to death and my mother's health is so bad now she had to move in with her sister in another state. I blame their misery on Conrad Oil."

"And you blame your own misery on my family, too," she said, unafraid of him now. "You understand, Hunter. It might hurt and you might not like it, but you're one of the few people who can find the truth on this." She stopped, took in a breath and wished she could blurt out all her findings. "In the same way you fought against my father to find out the truth about *your* sister's accident."

He took her by the arm, his expression brooding and brittle with rage. "I'll find the truth, all right. But you need to think long and hard on what's about to happen. I won't forgive and I won't forget. If I have to, I'll put them all in jail. So if you came here on some rich-girl mission to rebel against your daddy, you won't be having any fun."

Anger poured over Chloe in a heated rush. She glared up at him, matching the fire in his eyes. "Do I look like I'm having fun?"

He dropped her arm. "No."

Chloe saw the trace of regret in his stormy eyes and played on it. "If you can't find it in your heart to help me, then…I'll go home and keep digging on my own. I'm used to doing things on my own."

"And you'll die trying."

"Maybe. But at least I'll know I did my best."

He stared down at her, the battle raging inside him causing his body to shake. She could tell he wanted to say more, but before he could form the words, they heard tires hitting the shell-covered lane leading up to the house. Then headlights flashed briefly and went dark.

Hunter spun into action. Pushing her behind him, he pulled out his weapon and then hurried her around to the front of the house that faced the yard down to the beach.

"There's a path along the bay," he whispered. "I'm going to check this out, but if I'm not back in five minutes, take that path up to the road to the west. You'll find a bait shop there. Keep your phone close and call 911 if you think anyone is following you."

"I'm not going without you," she said, her nerves twisting into painful knots.

"You might not have any other choice," he said "Wait here. I should be back soon enough."

And then he was gone.

Chloe hid behind the storage room that wa

centered underneath the pilings and searched for anything she could use as a weapon. Determined not to leave without Hunter, she spotted a baseball bat. That could do some damage. She didn't want to think about what she'd do if Hunter got hurt. Or killed.

Hunter crouched low and moved through the shadows. Since he knew every shrub and tree in these woods, he had an advantage over whoever had come for a visit.

The battered pickup truck had stopped about halfway up the drive. He couldn't tell if anyone was inside or not and he didn't recognize the dark-colored truck.

When he heard the click of a gun being loaded, he went behind the truck and listened. Then he saw a man moving near the line of mossy oaks on one side of the driveway toward the house.

Hunter stayed behind him, following at a close distance. If this was part of the same hit team that had tried twice now, he'd have to take matters into his own hands. Whoever had sent them obviously wanted Chloe dead, no matter what.

The man was about ten yards away from the house when Hunter heard a buzzing sound. He stopped behind a massive live oak and listened after the man pulled out a cell phone.

"I think this is the place, but I don't see any-one around."

Silence. Hunter held his breath. How had they found Chloe here?

"Yeah, whatever, man. I need to get in, get out and go. And I'm not feeling this. Something's not right." Another pause. "Well, maybe he took her somewhere else." Then, "Yes, sir."

The man hung up and turned to head back to his truck.

Hunter met him, stepping out from the tree so quickly he tripped the unsuspecting man with a booted foot and then placed that same foot over the man's chest.

Aiming his Glock semiautomatic straight for the man's chest, he said, "Drop the gun and start talking."

Chloe checked her watch. Four minutes and counting. Now that the sun had gone down, i was hard to see past the palm trees and tower ing, moss-covered oaks. She didn't want to wall the dark path to the bait shop.

She wasn't going to, she decided. She woul go and find Hunter. With the old wooden ba held in a defensive mode in front of her, she ha just started around the storage room when sh heard footsteps approaching. She jumped bac and pressed against the wall, her breath stopping The footsteps kept coming.

Afraid to peek or to call out, Chloe held the bat up and waited. She heard a thump and then someone coming her way.

Bracing herself, she took a deep breath and held a death grip on the bat. Then she rushed around the corner of the storage room and made ready for battle.

The man took the bat right out of her hands.

"Hunter!"

He held the bat in one hand and her in the other. "What do you think you're doing?"

Chloe yanked away and straightened her clothes. "I was coming to look for you."

"With this?" He threw the bat down on the concrete floor and sent it rolling into a corner. "I see you're okay. That's good, at least."

"I'm fine. What happened?"

"He did," Hunter said, pointing to a skinny man with long stringy hair sitting with his hands caught up in a tight plastic ring of some sort. "He was looking for you."

Chloe walked over to the man and stared down at him. "Sonny?"

"You know this scumbag?" Hunter asked, his gaze swinging from her to the man.

"Yes," she said, sick to her stomach. "His name is Sonny Bolton. He works for my father."

Hunter walked over to where the man sat with downcast eyes. "Is that true?"

Sonny finally looked up, nodding to Chloe.

"Hey, Miss Chloe." Then he gave Hunter a look that bordered on fearful before he cast his gaze back on Chloe. "Mr. Conrad sent me to bring you home."

"Bring me home?" Shock filled Chloe's system. "Bring me home? What am I, a sack of potatoes?"

Sonny shrugged. "I don't know. I just follow orders."

Hunter leaned down eye-to-eye with Sonny. "Would those orders include trying to kill her? You were armed, remember?"

Sonny's head came up. "What? I don't know what you're talking about. I was told to find her, throw her in the truck and take off. Nobody said anything about killing anybody. I always travel with a weapon, and this place looked like I might need one."

Hunter got down on one knee and grabbed Sonny by the collar of his frayed button-up shirt. "Are you sure you didn't come here to hurt Miss Conrad?"

Sonny bobbed his head, his long neck stretching like a turkey's. "I'm not a killer. And why would I want to hurt Miss Chloe? She's always been good to me."

Chloe put a hand on Hunter's shoulder to rein him in. "Sonny, what are you doing here?"

"I told you, I came to get you. Your daddy

don't want you down here. He needs you to come home."

"Why didn't he just call and tell me that?" Chloe asked, thinking none of this made sense. Why would her father send Sonny down here when he could have sent a jet and any number of bodyguards?

Sonny shrugged again, his eyes downshifting. "I don't know."

"What do you know?" Hunter asked, lifting Sonny up and pushing him against the round wooden piling. "And don't even think about lying to me."

Sonny glanced at Chloe, appeal in his brown eyes. "Your daddy's been mighty worried about you. He gave me a wad of cash and told me to drive down here and locate you."

"And how did you find me?" Chloe asked.

Sonny's gaze shifted down the left. "I saw you on a motorcycle with him." He nodded toward Hunter. "Followed y'all to the Bay Road, saw where you turned in." He shrugged. "Plus, your daddy has a GPS on your phone, Miss Chloe. Led me right to you."

"Unbelievable," Chloe said. "Does he think I'm five years old or something?"

"Or something," Sonny mumbled, looking sheepish.

"What a stroke of luck," Hunter said, running

a hand over his hair. "I think I'll just put you on a boat and take you out a few miles to sea. And dump you. Shark bait."

Sonny swallowed and shook his head. "I'm just following orders."

Chloe glared at both of them. "Hunter, you can't hurt Sonny. He's been living on our land all his life. His family works for my daddy."

"What's that got to do with me dumping him in the bay?" Hunter asked, anger flaring in his eyes.

Sonny stood up straight. "I ain't never hurt nobody in my life and I'm not about to start now. I just want to get her home safe. Her daddy's stewing about something big and he's worried she's gonna get herself hurt."

Chloe pushed Hunter aside and put a hand on Sonny's arm. "Tell me why my father is so worried, Sonny."

Sonny gave her a beseeching look. "I can't say—"

And then they heard a pop and Sonny's eyes went wide. He slumped forward toward Chloe, one of his hands grabbing for her.

But Hunter caught him, realization registering on his face. He held his fingers to Sonny's neck.

"Chloe, he's dead."

"What?" Chloe reached for Sonny, a silent scream forming in her throat. "No." She tried to grab at the still man, but when she looked at his face she knew. As she looked down at Hunter's hand, she saw the blood seeping through Sonny's lightweight jacket and running over Hunter's fingers.

Sonny had been shot in the chest.

FOUR

Blain Kent scribbled on his pocket pad while the medical examiner and several uniformed officers moved around him.

Hunter rubbed his eyes and wished he hadn't brought Chloe here. This place was private and off-limits, but he'd been wrong to think it would be safe. He should have taken her somewhere way out from town. But where? He barely had a place to call his own. Just a small one-bedroom cottage near the marina. No way could he take her there.

Blain kept glancing up, questions hovering in his onyx eyes. The kind of questions he wouldn't want to answer in his official report.

Hunter would never hear the end of this.

Blain finished his notes and gave Hunter a long, puzzled stare. "What's next?"

Hunter didn't have the answer yet on that one. Well, he knew the answer and he didn't like it.

"Miss Conrad has hired me as her bodyguard," he said, his eyes clashing with Chloe's.

They hadn't discussed this, but he wasn't leaving her side now. This went beyond dealing with the Conrads. Someone was out to get her, no matter what. If her father had sent the now very dead Sonny Bolton to save her, he'd made a grave mistake. Why would a man who had millions send a grunt worker in a battered truck that had obviously come straight off some used-car dealer's lot to save his daughter? And how had the inept Sonny found this out-of-the-way hideaway?

None of this was adding up.

Neither was what Hunter had just offered. At the same time, he'd started this. Now he had to finish it.

She looked surprised at his words to Blain, but since she was still in shock over what had happened an hour ago, she didn't flinch.

"That's right," she said, her voice low but clear. "Obviously, someone is trying to stop me from investigating my sister's death. But I don't intend to stop. So I need…not only a bodyguard but a private investigator, too. Mr. Lawson seems to know what he's doing. He's kept me from possibly getting killed three times today."

She gave Hunter a grateful, shell-shocked glance.

"Of course." Blain's dark gaze flickered with

enlightenment and a touch of amazement. "Well, we've got both your statements and we've got people combing the woods and beach to look for the shooter. But I'm thinking he's long gone by now."

"Yeah, me, too," Hunter said. "Someone will be back, though. I need to get Miss Conrad to a safe place."

"I have a room at the Millbrook Inn," Chloe said. "I left a briefcase and a laptop there that I should pick up."

Blain gave Hunter another inquisitive glance. "Okay, then. Don't leave town for a couple of days, in case we need to question you again." Then he looked at Chloe. "We'll impound the victim's truck and go over it for any evidence. I can put a patrol car outside the inn, just in case."

Chloe nodded, her gaze holding Hunter's. He could almost read her thoughts. She needed to get back to Oklahoma.

They'd have to worry about that later. "I'll escort you to the inn and check your room," he said. Then he made another snap decision. "And I'll get a room there, too, if I have to. Nearby."

Blain didn't move a muscle and Hunter chafed under that dark detective gaze. He wanted to shout "It's not what you think." But he wasn't sure what to think himself. So he ignored Blain's steady, all-knowing scrutiny and focused on what needed to be done.

Then he turned back to Chloe. "Will that work for now?"

"Yes," she said, a hint of relief and surprise in her voice.

"Hunter, a word please." Blain's quizzical expression had changed to one of concern.

"Sure." Hunter didn't want to have this conversation because Blain would want too many answers. And right now, Hunter would rather have his teeth pulled out than explain all of this to anyone. But he walked a few feet away with Blain, his gaze on Chloe. She turned to stare out at the moonlight over the bay.

"Uh, what's going on?" Blain asked, his pen tapping his notepad. "Off the record."

Hunter shrugged. "It's a long story." Blain had said that same thing to him once, regarding getting involved with Rikki Alvanetti, so Hunter hoped his friend would cut him some slack.

"I might need to hear it. You could be in with some real dangerous people, bro."

"Tell me something I don't know," Hunter replied. "She showed up at the Hog Wash and then someone took a shot at us and it's been one big adventure since then." Had that only been a few hours ago?

Blain leaned close. "This was an execution.

Probably by a professional. Why didn't you call in the attack at the Hog Wash?"

Hunter knew better. "I should have, but the owner didn't want the attention and I had to act fast. You know how that place operates. The Hog Wash is like a haven for misfits and people of questionable repute."

"So that's why you always hang out there," Blain said with a tight smile. "Makes perfect sense."

"Funny," Hunter said, glad for the levity. "It was a judgment call. One I'm regretting now."

Blain nodded. "Yes, because we could have tried to trace the shooter."

Hunter wasn't one to argue about the rules. "I agree. But there were no witnesses. It was her and me out on the deck, and since they used a silencer, we only heard a ping and then the car sped away. I didn't get a good look and I didn't see the license plate on the vehicle."

He described the car and Blain said he'd make a note in what would be a long report on this shooting.

"Look, Blain, let me do what I need to do to get her back to Oklahoma safe and sound. She's scared and she doesn't trust her own father right now."

Blain glanced over at Chloe and then gave

Hunter a steady gaze. "I trust *you*. So you be careful and let me know if you need my help."

"I will," Hunter said, meaning it. He'd never trusted anyone easily, but Blain was one person he knew he could depend on. "I'm taking her to the inn and we'll decide what our next move is."

"You can't take off to Oklahoma in the middle of the night," Blain reminded him. "Not just yet, okay?"

"Got it," Hunter said. He wasn't used to getting so involved with the locals, but he knew the law. He didn't want to get on Blain's bad side. "I'll keep her here for a few days and try to piece things together."

After Blain and his men finished up, Hunter walked over to Chloe. "Let's go."

"Your friend doesn't like me," she commented as they walked to his bike.

"He doesn't know you," Hunter said. "Big difference."

"I've brought danger to his town."

"Yeah, but don't be so melodramatic. He's good at his job. And he can be an asset to us if we need him."

"He doesn't want me to leave, so that means he suspects me of something."

"It's a detective's nature to suspect people."

They got on the motorcycle and zoomed toward the dark road. Hunter checked the landscape and hoped they wouldn't be attacked anymore tonight.

Chloe held tightly to him, giving him that odd sensation again. Something about this woman's touch got to him.

That led to another revelation.

He truly wanted to protect her.

Blain was right about one thing at least. This had become dangerous. In more ways than just being shot at.

An hour later, Chloe sat in a secluded corner where Hunter had deposited her away from the many doors and windows in the Millbrook Lake Inn. After he'd made sure no strange cars were in the tiny parking lot or out on the street and explained to the surprised desk clerk what he was doing, he came back to stand over Chloe.

"Patrol car's out front," he said in his stern, no-nonsense voice. "And the officer is guarding the front door and patrolling the parking lot. Don't move. I'll be back in a few."

The woman everyone called Miss Ida smiled as he headed up the wide staircase just past the check-in desk. "Even though Hunter explained he needed to check your room before you go inside, I'm not sure what's going on but if you're with him, you're in good hands. That's one tall drink of water."

Chloe couldn't think about that tall drink of water right then. She swallowed back her fear and prayed Hunter wouldn't find anything wrong upstairs. "He's…uh…helping me with a problem."

Miss Ida pursed her thin lips. "Yes, ma'am. I don't ask questions. That's your business."

"No, no, it's not like that," Chloe said, wishing she could get up and walk around. "I mean, he's not a…friend. We just met."

"Right." Miss Ida shuffled some papers. "That's Hunter Lawson, baby. We all know about him. He is a man of few words but big on action from what we hear around here. Served our country in some sort of elite, secretive capacity and now he's decided to live here in Millbrook Lake."

"Yes, ma'am, so I've heard."

That was one of the reasons she'd hired him. Because he was the kind of person you wanted in your corner. Laura must have thought so. Why else would she have jotted his name in her notes? And now that she'd met Hunter, Chloe could certainly understand why Miss Ida beamed with almost motherly pride.

Thinking of how much she missed her mother right now, Chloe pushed away her doubts regarding her father. She had to find out who killed Laura and she prayed their father hadn't been involved in any of this.

Please, Lord, don't let anything else bad hap-

pen to the people I care about. Or to the man I hired.

Miss Ida shuffled around the desk, her hand patting her silvery white bob. She wore a blue cashmere turtleneck and black pants with a snazzy pair of black pointed-toe loafers. "Can I get you anything?"

"No, thank you," Chloe said.

"Can I pray for you?"

Chloe wanted to hug this sweet woman tight. "Yes. That's the best thing you can do for me right now."

The older woman touched Chloe's hand and sent her a peaceful smile. "I'm on it."

Chloe sank against the big chair and inhaled the smell of something spicy-sweet wafting out from the diffuser on a nearby table. This was a beautiful place, Victorian and rambling, with elegant antique furnishings and big, cozy rooms. But Chloe couldn't enjoy being here.

Hunter had told her they'd get in, get what she needed and move on. But where he'd take her, she didn't know.

He'd grilled the sweet clerk and through it all Miss Ida had remained calm and explained that she hadn't seen any strange cars or any mysterious men. Chloe hoped she could leave without getting this lovely old place shot up. She certainly didn't want Miss Ida or any of the other guests to get hurt.

Hunter came barreling back down the stairs, his gaze moving from her to the very curious Miss Ida. "You can come up now."

He didn't speak again until they were inside the room. "Did you have anything in the safe?"

"Yes. And on the table." Chloe grabbed the briefcase she'd left on the mahogany table near the French doors. "This is still locked. Is the safe?"

"No," he said, guiding her to the closet. "I didn't want to say anything downstairs, but the safe is open and empty."

Chloe stared into the closet. "I think they found what they wanted. My laptop was in there."

Hunter let out a frustrated breath. "They must have zoomed in on the safe with a grab-and-go. Must have seen us coming since they left the briefcase. But you said you made copies of part of the information and stored those copies in a secure place?"

She lifted her chin. "I did, but now I think you're right. No place is safe. And *I'll* never be safe again, either."

"All the more reason to put you in hiding," he said. "Grab your things. We're getting out of here."

Chloe found her overnight bag and shoved her

clothes and toiletry items in it and zipped it. "I didn't bring much," she said. "I'm ready."

Hunter took the big leather bag and she held on to her briefcase and her purse. "My laptop had a lot of other files I could use—work-related documents and my contact list."

"Too bad," he said, guiding her down the back stairs to the big courtyard surrounded by banana trees and sago palms.

Hunter opened the wrought-iron gate and slid around the corner. "We need to ditch my bike and get my truck."

Chloe couldn't argue with that. "Where is your truck?"

"About a half mile to the east at my place near the marina."

"Think we can make it without being shot at?"

"I doubt it."

He kept her near the bushes and trees, his gaze moving along the street by the inn. "I'm going to put you in the patrol car and let the officer follow me to my place. We'll switch out vehicles there, okay?"

"Okay." Curious to see where he lived, Chloe followed him through the shadows to the parked cruiser out on the curb.

When they got close, Hunter did a knuckle knock on the driver's-side window. "He has to be inside since I didn't see him walking the perimeters."

He found the officer slumped over the steering wheel.

Hunter turned and shoved Chloe forward. "Run!" he shouted, pointing to the road toward the marina. "Run, Chloe, and don't look back."

FIVE

Chloe held tight to her shoulder bag and briefcase and took off running up the sideway toward
the marina located on one of the curves of the
lake. But where was Hunter?

She glanced back and saw Hunter close on her
heels.

With two men chasing him.

He caught up with her and shoved her into
some oleander bushes. "Go," he said. "Shortcut
across the park."

He took her briefcase and they kept running
until he pulled her up into a sandy driveway shadowed by tall palms on each side. "We're at my
place," he said. "I dropped your overnight bag
back at the inn. Used it to trip one of them up."

"It's okay. Nothing I can't replace." She was
out of breath, but at least they seemed to be safe
for now.

Hunter kept her in front of him and glanced
back over his shoulder as he whisked her up the

steps leading to a small covered deck. "This should buy us some time. They might have figured out I live here already so we need to hurry."

"Another house on stilts," she said, taking in the whitewashed shingles covering the side of the house.

"A necessity in hurricane country."

He opened a side door and led her in. "Stay away from the windows."

Chloe knew the drill. She scanned a galley kitchen and a big square room that contained a bed and living area with a bathroom off the back. Very sterile and stark. No room for anything lasting.

But she couldn't analyze the house right now. "Will they ever stop?"

"No," he said. "Give me your phone."

She found her phone in her crossover bag. "The GPS? I didn't check it earlier."

"I'm thinking it's more than a GPS."

He kept looking out the window, her phone in his hand.

With the light from one muted lamp, he scrolled through her apps. "Just what I thought. Someone has put a spyware app on your phone."

"What?" Chloe rushed over to stare at her phone. "How could that happen?"

"It's not that hard," he said. "If you left it on

your desk or let someone use it for just a couple of minutes, they could easily set this up."

"I left it on my desk at work," she said, her mind overflowing with several scenarios. "Any number of people could have had access to it."

He showed her a map he'd pulled up. "They've tracked your every move, beginning with your private flight and the rental car and look." He pointed to a red dot on the map. "Here's the Mill-brook Inn."

Chloe let out a gasp. "Then that means they're on their way here now. They know where we are right now."

"Yes." He deleted the app and then he took her phone and dropped it on the floor. "You have several missed calls and messages from some-one named Bridget. You'll have to wait on get-ting back to her."

"Okay," Chloe said. She'd seen the messages, but she hadn't had a chance to check in with her overly protective friend. Bridget worked for Con-rad Oil, too, as Chloe's assistant. Bridget knew almost as much about the company as Chloe did, since she shadowed Chloe and scheduled her days.

Which was probably the main reason Chloe was avoiding her. She didn't want to get Bridget involved any more than she already was.

Hunter kicked the phone toward the sofa.

"That should throw them off for a while. We have to go."

He hurried her down to where a big black truck was parked behind the house. Before she could get in, he swung the door open and lifted her up onto the seat and then he ran around to the driver's side and got in.

Chloe ignored the sensations that had shot through her when he'd placed her inside the truck. Strength mixed with steel. That was him. A man of steel. Superman? No, just a man who'd hardened himself against the world.

But his touch had been gentle.

Spinning tires and spewing dirt made the big vehicle sound as if it was growling, but Hunter got them out of the yard and through a back alley.

"So far, so good."

They were headed along the Bay Road out from town when Hunter noticed a car tailing them too close. He glanced in the rearview mirror, but he didn't say anything to Chloe.

When the car sped up and did a bold tap against the back bumper, he shifted into overdrive. "I'm taking you to the safest place I know," he told Chloe. "Hold on."

Chloe grabbed the door and glanced back. "What's wrong?"

"Oh, just a tailgater getting a little too close."

"They're after us again, aren't they?"

"I think so."

Hunter watched as the pickup backed off. But he knew what was coming next. The truck came at them again. When he heard the shot, he braced for the worst, his right hand automatically reaching for Chloe. "Get down."

She screamed and leaned forward.

But the shooter wasn't trying to hit either of them.

He'd gone for one of the tires.

And now Hunter's truck was spinning out of control.

Hunter gritted his teeth and held on to the wheel, letting the truck do what it had to do before he could get it back into control. Once he'd righted it, he'd done a complete one-eighty turn and was now facing the truck idling a few yards away.

"Are you all right?" he asked Chloe. He pulled his gun out and readied it.

"Yes." She sat up and glanced over at him. "Hunter?"

"Keep holding on," he said. "Time to play chicken."

"What are you doing?" Chloe held so tightly to the door handle she thought her knuckles would crack. "Hunter?"

"Just hang on," he said, the grit in his words

enough to warn her to stay quiet. "Get down in the seat."

He let down his window and held the gun close to the opening while he revved the engine, making the big truck roar with power. Then he hit the gas pedal and headed straight for the truck that had tried to run them down, firing bullets all the way. "I'll show these idiots how it's supposed to be done."

Chloe took in a deep breath and closed her eyes, willing her body to curl in a tight ball as she tried to stay out of the line of fire. They were going to crash into the idling vehicle. Even with one bad tire, the Chevy ate up the space between them and the people who'd chased them.

Return fire popped and sizzled all around the Chevy.

She opened her eyes for a fraction of a second and peeked over the dash, a scream wedged inside her throat. Bracing herself for the crash, she thought about Laura and wondered why in the world she thought she could trust this man. He was as full of rage as her late stepbrother.

And then at the last second, the other truck jerked to the left so hard and fast the driver couldn't right it as he tried to swerve away. The vehicle hit the soft earthy drop-off leading down into the bay and went over, dirt spraying out behind it and the smell of burning rubber lifting up into the air.

Chloe held her breath, her eyes on Hunter. He slammed on the brakes and stopped the truck, his right hand still on the steering wheel. His gun still aimed out the door.

"I guess we won that round," he said on a low growl. Then he turned to stare over at her. "How ya doing over there?"

Chloe wanted to laugh. She wanted to cry. "You scared me."

"I had to stop them, one way or another."

She nodded and finally let go of the door, her hands shaking so badly she gave up and held them together in her lap.

He watched her in that quiet, dangerous way that unnerved Chloe. But she wouldn't fall apart now.

"What's next?" she asked, swiping at her hair.

"Do you know how to change a tire?"

Amazed that he somehow made her smile in spite of what they'd just been through, she said, "As a matter of fact, I do."

His look of surprise was replaced with one of admiration. "It's okay. I was messing with you. That flat tire is evidence. We can't touch it."

"What about them?" she asked, looking back toward the road behind them.

"Not my problem."

"Aren't you going to report them?"

"Eventually."

He got out and came around to her side of the truck and opened the door, his dark gaze scanning her until he seemed satisfied that she wasn't hurt. Then he handed her the gun. "Stay here while I make sure we're safe. Shoot anything that moves."

Chloe did as he said. He turned and stalked over to the bay side of the curving road and stared down into what looked like a thicket of scrub brush and palmetto palms. Then he pulled out his phone. She heard him giving details, so he must have called someone official.

He came back to stand by her and he took back his gun. "The truck's halfway submerged in the shallows, but I can't tell if they're still in it or not. They probably got out and ran up toward the beach area. I reported the accident, so I'll have to stay here and give a statement to the police."

"I have to get out of here," Chloe said. "But do I go back to Oklahoma and start all over?"

"It's not safe there, but we'll come up with a plan."

"We need to keep moving."

"I know," he said. "And this could take a while, but if I'm going to be your official bodyguard, you need to wait here with me for now, understand?"

She didn't like having to wait, but she did like the part where he'd accepted being her bodyguard. "I'll wait."

"I'll try to hurry things along," he said.

She stared out into the distance where the crescent moon hung over the bay like a bright lantern. "Should I call my dad and play coy?"

"No. They might have a tracking device or a tracer on his phone, too."

"They know where I am already, Hunter."

"But they don't know if we have any new information or not. You can't talk to him right now. Or anyone else, either. I'm sorry."

Chloe didn't protest. When they heard sirens echoing from the east, she gave Hunter one last glance. "I hope those men run into some sharks out there."

He nodded and took off to meet the ambulance and the cruiser.

Chloe thought she probably should have told him that Bridget knew why she was here and that she would have a hissy fit once she found out what had been going on. How could she tell her nervous Nellie friend that she'd been shot at and chased since she arrived in Florida early this morning? Even though she'd helped Chloe track down Hunter, Bridget had warned her against this trip. But Hunter had been her last hope.

Now she'd put him in danger, too. When would this ever end?

The only glimmer of hope came from Hunter actually witnessing this attack. He believed her when no one else would.

Thank You, Lord.

Right now Hunter had his hands full. She'd tell him later about everyone who knew she was here and about what she'd found in Laura's notes. Once they were away from this swamp-infested curve in the road, she'd be able to think about who might want her dead.

Because she'd never believe her father was behind this.

Hunter's work sometimes involved talking to the locals and filing reports, but tonight he didn't have the stomach for the mundane part of being a private investigator.

He needed to get Chloe somewhere safe. This road was too isolated and too exposed for her to be sitting here in the dark.

So he hurried things up with the two patrolmen and then called Blain to give him an update and waited to see what the first responders had found in the dense foliage along the hillside down to the bay.

"The vehicle is empty," he heard one of the EMTs telling the responding officer. "We checked all around. One door is open, so if anyone was inside, they either managed to get out or they drowned."

Hunter had heard enough. He'd done all he could here and he didn't need to be in on any further searches. His truck had been moved off the road. The tow truck could have it for now to take in as evidence.

He made a call to Alec and then opened the passenger-side door and looked into Chloe's wide eyes. "C'mon. I've got a friend coming to give us a ride to a safe place."

She took the hand he offered and hopped down. "You seem to have a lot of friends."

"Just three that I can count on."

She didn't ask any more questions. They stood by the truck, the damp cold night air surrounding them while the water lapped at the shore down below.

"Those men got away, didn't they?" she asked, a shiver tapping down her spine. "There had to be at least two, right? One driver and one gunman."

He leaned down and swiped at his bangs. "You must watch a lot of crime shows."

"I'm just being logical."

"Yeah, you're probably right. These kinds of underlings always travel in pairs."

"And the ones who first showed up at the bar would have taken me or shot me right there if you hadn't been there with me," she said. "But you stopped them."

"You should have stayed in Oklahoma and let the locals figure this out."

"The locals don't care."

He gave her a hard stare, but his whisper was raw and low. "And you think I do?"

His question hadn't fooled her. She stared up at him with wide-open eyes. "I know you do. You've proven that over and over today."

She had him there, but Hunter wasn't ready to concede. "I didn't have much of a choice. I couldn't let you get hurt or worse. I won't have that on my conscience."

"You're right," she said, a cold disappointment cresting in her expression. "You were just doing your job."

Thankfully, Alec pulled up in a sleek SUV and saved Hunter from having to analyze things too deeply. Best to just go with it and not think about how this woman was cramping his style and messing with his head.

"Ride's here," he said, taking her by the arm to put her in the backseat.

Chloe gave him a questioning look as she got in the vehicle but she didn't say anything.

Hunter got in the front. "Alec Caldwell, meet Chloe Conrad."

Alec turned around and offered his hand. "Nice to meet you. Sorry about the circumstances."

Chloe stared at his extended hand for a moment and then shook it. He was different from Hunter. More clean-cut and upper-crust. "Same here. Thank you for helping us."

"You're welcome," Alec said. Then he turned and faced Hunter. "Where to?"

"About that, bro," Hunter said. "We need one more favor, but it's a big one."

SIX

Chloe couldn't believe Hunter had brought her here, of all places. But she hadn't had time to argue, since he'd insisted they had to hide her until he could come up with a plan.

He'd asked Alec Caldwell to let her stay in the training dorms at a place called Caldwell Canines Service Dog Association. It was a big industrial building on the outskirts of town, surrounded by security fences and a well-lit parking lot and training yard.

The preacher—their other friend they'd also called—a nice man named Rory Sanderson, escorted Chloe to one of the dorm rooms and set her suitcase on the luggage rack before he scanned the area outside the small window. "You should be safe here. Your room faces the training yard."

Chloe glanced around at the stark but clean room, which contained a single bed, a cushioned side chair and a small functional dresser/desk combo with a tiny flat-screen television and a narrow closet. A small bath was off to the side. When Hunter had suggested she stay in one of the dorm rooms here, she'd been surprised. But now she was beginning to understand. Alec had readily agreed.

"So this is the Caldwell Canines Service Dog Association?"

Rory Sanderson's smile lit up. Giving her a blue-eyed gaze, he said, "The official name is the Alexander and Vivian Caldwell Service Dog Association. But that's a lot to remember. We call it Caldwell Canines for short."

He pointed to the area beyond the second-story window. "Clients who are in need of a service dog are screened for acceptance, but this organization rarely turns anyone away. Clients come here to train with a dog matched to their needs. Most of the dogs are pound animals, so a lot of them live here on the property until they can be matched with a human. Funding covers scholarships for those who can't pay their own way."

He stopped and grinned again. "Sorry. I'm on the board of directors, so I have to give that spiel to everyone I meet."

"Interesting," Chloe said, the distraction taking her mind off her troubles for a brief time. She closed her eyes and prayed that Hunter would stay safe. He'd gone back to the bay to search for the two men who'd tried to kill them.

"It's a win-win situation," Rory said. "People come here from all over the country, a lot of them wounded veterans, and work with the staff and the animals. I've seen a lot of amazing things happen in this place. These dogs learn to do all kinds of everyday tasks, but I think it's the unconditional love that cures our wounded warriors more than anything."

Chloe smiled at that. "Animals can sense things like that, right?"

"Right." Rory gave her a patient, understanding stare. He probably thought she needed lots of prayers and maybe a puppy, too.

She heard dogs barking, but the big yard looked deserted. "I don't see anyone training out there," she said, numbness and apprehension tugging at her. She certainly didn't want to stay in this big place all by herself.

"Alec said they'd just finished a session. But there is an entire staff here around the clock and most of them are trained in either K-9 work or service dog expertise. And if anyone unknown walks up onto the property, the dogs will all start barking."

She had to smile at that. "Hunter brought me to a place that is covered by a lot of watchdogs?"

"Hunter has a wry sense of humor and a strong sense of duty."

She could agree with that. "I hope he finds the people responsible for all this."

Rory turned from the window and gave her another quiet stare. "Hunter is good at his job and he has a knack for sniffing out bad people. If anyone can solve this puzzle, it'll be Hunter Lawson."

"That's why I came across the country to hire him," she admitted. "I'll be fine here if you and Hunter vouch for this place." She hung her jacket across the chair. "And Alec assured me this is okay. I got the feeling he's here a lot."

"He's devoted to the cause," Rory said. "And his PR assistant had to move to the West Coast with her air force husband, so he's doing double duty for a few weeks until he finds someone to replace her."

"That is devoted." Chloe imagined working here could be very rewarding.

"Okay, then. A few things to know."

Rory showed her the small bathroom connected to her room and then took her to meet some of the staff members and showed her the kitchen and dining area and the lounge where a television, magazines and books were located, and explained the Wi-Fi hotspots to her but suggested she didn't get on the internet for her own protection.

"Stay on the premises and mostly in the training yard," he told her. "This place has tight security. It's well lit and it has a state-of-the-art alarm system. We'll all come by and check on you around the clock, and knowing Hunter, he'll find someone he can trust to sit right outside your room. You can also alert the staff at any time, day or night."

"*Who* will come by?" she asked. "I need to know what to expect."

Again, that patient smile. "Me," Rory said. "Alec and probably his wife, Marla, Blain and his wife, Rikki, if she's in town, and my fiancée, Vanessa. She'll force you to look at wedding stuff and she'll go on and on about her dress and the food and how much she loves me but just humor her, okay?"

Chloe liked the preacher. She smiled and nodded. "Okay. I don't mind looking at wedding stuff or hearing how in love your fiancée is with you. I think that's sweet."

He grinned over at her. "It's a girl thing, right?"

"Right."

Rory said a prayer with her and then gave her a preacherly hug and a pledge to pray for her. "Call if you need anything."

She waved bye to him and took some clothes and toiletries out of her suitcase, but Chloe couldn't relax. She felt as if she'd been relegated to a nice prison. Rubbing her hands down her arms, she tried to stay calm, but her skin crawled with fear and anger and dread while her pulse pounded against her temple like a warning bell that wouldn't stop. She needed all the prayers people were promising.

What if they didn't find those men?

What if something bad happened to Hunter or one of his friends? When would they be able to sit down and really get to the bottom of this? What if Hunter left her here and took off on his own?

What if…

She finally sat down on the bed and had a good cry. Followed by serious prayers. She missed her sister, Laura, so much. Laura had been completely solid in her faith, so sure that the world still had some good in it. Chloe had doubted. Her faith was more lukewarm and shaky. But she had to admit, when she'd seen Hunter's name scrawled in Laura's notes, she'd considered it a sure sign from God.

So why couldn't she tell him everything? Why couldn't she tell him that he might be more involved in this than he realized?

Hunter would have been the last person she'd think of in a time such as thing. But Laura had obviously thought of him.

"Laura, help me to find the answers," she

whispered. Then she asked God to guide her. "And…please, Lord, protect Hunter."

Chloe squared her shoulders and sank down in the chair across from the bed. She thought she'd smoothed things over with her father before she left by telling him she needed to get away for a few days, but her father had a way of discovering the truth. He didn't know she'd come here to find Hunter Lawson. She'd told him she was coming to Florida for a getaway trip, since she'd been working overtime for the last few months. Had her father really tracked her here and tried to have her killed?

No. Wayne Conrad was a hard, stubborn, powerful man, but he'd never kill one of his own children. He'd been mourning the loss of his only son for years now and then Laura had died, too. Her horrible death had been hard on all of them.

Lately, her father had lost focus on the vast empire he'd created. Tray had been a mean alcoholic drug abuser who'd beaten his wife and controlled every aspect of her short life. But her father had never given up hope that Tray would get clean and have a good life one day.

Hunter's older sister, Beth, had loved Tray in spite of all of that. She'd never managed to break away from the hold Tray had over her.

But Hunter had avenged her death and put Tray in prison.

Wayne Conrad hated Hunter Lawson.

Chloe sat up and put her hand over her mouth. Laura had written Hunter's name down in her notes. Had there been more to that than just wanting him to help her? She'd have to come clean with Hunter one day but not right now. It was too dangerous to even mention the theory she had developed when she couldn't sleep at night.

"Daddy, did you send those men after me? Or did you send them to kill Hunter?"

When she heard a knock on the door, Chloe's pulse spiked into overdrive.

"Who is it?" she asked before opening the door.

"Hunter."

Chloe grabbed the doorknob and let him in, her hands shaking, her heart skipping and jumping. "Did you find them? Did you find the people who're trying to kill us?"

"No, but I will find them. All of them."

Hunter held his hands on Chloe's arms while he tried to reassure her. She felt tiny and fragile, but there was muscle underneath her slender frame. He saw that shard of steel in her eyes and that caused him to worry about her even more. He did not want to worry about her. Or this mess.

But he couldn't walk away now. This was getting serious. Too serious. They're tried to get to

Chloe by every means possible, and now they'd upped things a notch.

They'd contacted *him* with a warning.

A dangerous warning.

He didn't tell her about the cryptic phone call he'd received once he left her with Rory. Plenty of time for that later. She needed to rest and stay calm right now.

"Tell Chloe Conrad to go back to Oklahoma before she loses everyone she loves."

Just that and then nothing. But Hunter had heard what sounded like a boat's motor revving in the background and the sound of the water taxi horn blowing to indicate it was leaving the public docks. Those docks were a few blocks from here.

The first clue.

"Hunter, what's going on?"

"Nothing. We haven't found anything. No prints, no weapons, no humans." He sat her down in the chair and then he sank back on the end of the bed, exhaustion weighing him down. "But we found your laptop in a ditch. Someone had shot holes in it."

Chloe gripped the wooden arms of her chair, her expression full of regret and fear. "I should have stayed there and done this on my own. I shouldn't have brought you into this."

Hunter wished she hadn't come to him, either, but his reasons had nothing to do with someone trying to off him. Now in spite of his feelings regarding her, he wasn't about to let her out of his sight. "Well, you're here now and I'm in it with you. And that means I'm with you twenty-four-seven for the next few days."

"But we need to get back to Oklahoma and see what we can find."

"We'll do that, but for now we build a case that shows your sister could possibly have been murdered. We'll need to set up a time frame of the days before her death and try to find anyone she might have spoken with."

She stood up, her gaze downcast. "I need something to focus on. I'll use the computers here sparingly, but wish I had my laptop."

"Trust me, that machine is stone-cold dead. Blain took it as evidence, but it's fried." Hunter motioned to the door. "Let's go to the break room and get some coffee and a snack," he suggested.

This little room was too closed-in and tight for him. It put him too close to her. He needed some air.

"Okay." She got up, worry shadowing her face. "Hunter, I had a thought while you were gone."

"Yeah, and what was that?"

She held her hands twisted together in front of her. "If these people tracked me all the way here, they could easily have taken me the minute the plane landed or right after I got the rental car, but they didn't."

He nodded. "That did cross my mind. They've had several opportunities to either kidnap you or kill you and they could have come after you back in Oklahoma. But they didn't."

"And yet they waited until I was that restaurant, hoping to find you."

"Somebody is definitely stirred up," he said. "Maybe they were waiting for the perfect opportunity."

"Or maybe they were waiting for something else," she replied. "Someone else."

Hunter saw the reality of her words in her eyes. Before he could voice what he was thinking, she did it for him.

"What about you?" she asked, a dark dread in her eyes.

Chloe gulped in a breath and dropped her hands down by her side. She didn't speak for a moment and he didn't try to encourage her. Hunter saw things in black and white. There were no gray areas in his mind. So there was no point in stating the obvious.

Finally, her gaze locked with his and her eyes went wide with anguish. "What if they're not after *me*, Hunter? What if they tracked me here so they could kill *you*?"

SEVEN

Hunter walked to the window and stared out at the glow from the yellow security lights. Could she be right?

"I don't believe that," he said. "Why would anyone be after me now? I haven't been to Oklahoma in a long time."

"You left Oklahoma under a dark cloud," she said. "My father never got over seeing his only son go to prison, but I can't see him doing this. He understood your need to find the truth even if he didn't agree with you."

"He tried to cover up the truth," Hunter said, wondering if she even realized what an evil man her father truly was. "But he'd know better than to send someone to take me out. Besides, he's had three years to do that and I've been right here all that time. I think someone just followed you to make a point. And somehow I'm now along for the ride."

Chloe paced the confines of the little room

"Think about it. I came across the country to find you. If someone had access to my phone long enough to put that spyware on it, they could easily have checked my calls, my texts and my search history."

He whirled and reached for her arm. "Did you research me before you came here?"

"Yes," she said, lifting his hand away. "I always do my homework. I knew of you, of course, but I needed current information on you. My mother followed the news reports about your sister's death, so I was already familiar with you. I found even more information online and in the library archives back home."

She cast her gaze down again. What was she hiding?

"But no one there really knew where I'd gone," he said, an uncomfortable realization settling in his brain. "I didn't hide it. I just didn't announce it, either. But you said Gerald Howard told you where I was?"

"Not really. I'd heard you went to work as a PI under his guidance and that he helped you train so you could get your license. I went to him, asking about you, since you and he had been friends before—"

"Before he took your father's side, you mean."

"Gerald also knew my brother, so he felt obligated. He told me you two had lost touch. He didn't seem to know where you were."

"He's only obligated to money, and your father paid him a hefty salary to do his dirty work. So my former friend and boss was working against me the whole time I was working to find out what really happened on that country road the night my sister died. Tray got away with murder until I found out the truth and forced your father to see that truth. Why don't we talk about *Tray* and see if we can hit on anything your father might still be holding against me?"

She turned to face Hunter. "Tray was just a boy when my father divorced his mother and married mine. My sister and I weren't around Tray that much, since he lived with his mother, so none of us ever got close to him. After Tray started drinking in his late teens, our mother wanted to protect us from him and…a lot of other things…so she left my father when we were still young. By that time, Tray was twenty-one and on his own."

Hunter's gut burned with disgust. "And then a few years later he met Beth and…you know the rest of the story."

"Yes. We all know the rest of the story." She turned to stare down at the enclosed yard. "Tray was an alcoholic and he was unstable. I can't change what he did to Beth and I can't bring either of them back, but you might be surprised to know I agree with what you did. You fought my family to prove it wasn't an accident, and because of your efforts, Tray went to prison for vehicular manslaughter."

"Yep." Hunter couldn't even speak about Tray Conrad. Hatred still burned in his gut like a raw, out-of-control fire, and standing here with this woman was only bringing it all back to the surface. "Beth was the best a person could be, so him going to prison didn't change anything. It didn't bring her back." He took a deep breath. "And we're not getting anywhere rehashing what we can't change."

Chloe pivoted and leaned against the wall by the window, her eyes on him. "No, but what you did took a lot of courage. And I'm glad you fought for your sister. That's why I came to you, Hunter. I knew you'd fight for *my* sister, too."

"What makes you think I care?" he said, wanting to hurt her. Needing to put some distance between him and her. "You and your sister weren't even around. I never knew you because you were living away with your mama, and I left right after things came to a head."

He didn't like the way he sounded, but he wouldn't give in to her false adoration for him. She didn't know him. How was it that she agreed with him and supported what he'd done, when his own family and most of his friends had turned on him? When his own mother had left Oklahoma and moved to Arkansas because of all the unwanted exposure the trial had brought. At least she was safe there, living with her younger sister.

Chloe leaned against the wall and tugged the black sweater she'd changed into around her. "Yes, but my mother talked about the wreck and read out loud from the news articles on the investigation and the trial. I heard it all each time I came home from college." Staring up at him, she shook her head. "I think I became enamored with you just from hearing those news reports. And then—"

Hunter moved in front of her and placed one hand on the wall by her head. "You can't be serious? If you came here looking for a hero, you've wasted your time. Don't pin your hopes on me, because you don't know me. There is nothing romantic or endearing about what I did. It was torment and stubbornness—that's what got me through it. Don't make it into anything more. You have no idea about any of this."

Chloe nodded, pushed at her hair. "No, I don't, but I do know you. And I know about Tray, too. Mother left my father because of Tray and she lives in Texas now. Our daddy babied him and spoiled him even more after his mother died. He always put Tray first. But I knew…even though I'd never met you, that you were right. My older stepbrother could have done this on purpose. I was around a couple of times when he'd gone into one of his drunken rages. He had a horrible disease, Hunter. And it finally caught up with him when he died in prison last year."

She stared up at him with those golden-brown diamond eyes, her heart and her hope right there between them. "Yes, Tray is gone now. He died an awful death, locked up and alone. But I'm here and I do know you and I know what you went through. I believe you can help me. And if I'm right about these people and they did come for you, too, then we need each other. We need to figure this out together."

"No," Hunter replied, his own rage resurfacing. "No, a disease is like cancer or heart trouble. He was a stinking drunk and a drug user and he killed Beth. Killed her because she'd had enough of his brutality and cruelty…and because she had finally found the courage to leave him. Dying in prison wasn't any kind of punishment for him. But I guess it does rank right up there with rotting in prison."

He lifted his hand off the wall and paced to the other side of the little room. "I've had enough and now you show up and come up with this theory about them wanting *me* dead, too. What more do you Conrads expect from me?"

"You appointed yourself my bodyguard," she

reminded him. "Have you changed your mind now that you might be in danger?"

"I don't care about being in any danger," he retorted with a sense of disdain. "I can take care of myself, but now I have to take care of you, too."

And what if he couldn't do that? Hunter couldn't live with one more death on his mind. He'd had enough of war and death and revenge. "I just want some peace and quiet."

Chloe studied him, strength and defiance in her expression. "We'd all had enough," she said, as if she'd been inside his head. "Don't you think it's time to try and make it right once and for all? Help me find the same kind of justice for my sister that you found for Beth. Help me to find justice for both of us."

Moving closer, she added, "Please, Hunter, don't back out on me now. Not after you told me you'd find these people. If you do, neither of us will ever be completely free again."

"I don't see how that'll make anything even," he retorted. "I'll never be rid of the mighty Conrads, no matter what I do." And because he had to test her and maybe torment her, he got in her face again. "Or did you purposely come here to do me in?"

Shock registered on her face. "You think I set this up? Really? After the time we've had?"

"You tell me, Chloe. Since the moment I laid

eyes on you, I've been shot at and hounded by people who seem very determined and now you decide they might be after me, too. For all I know, you could be using your sister's death as an excuse to finally get revenge for your grieving father."

"That's not true. There's something else you need to know."

"Yeah, and what's that? When will you really tell me the truth?"

"This is the truth," she said. "I have another very good reason for seeking you out. My sister had written your name in her notes. In big, bold letters. *Hunter Lawson*, with a question mark beside it. I thought she wanted to hire you so I found you. But what if she wanted to warn you, too?"

Hunter couldn't believe what he'd just heard. "Why didn't you tell me that right up front?"

"Because we've been kind of busy trying to stay alive."

She pushed away, disgust evident in the glare of her eyes. "I can leave right now. I was concerned about you, so I told you what I'd been thinking, but if you're too mule-headed to protect yourself, then have at it. You seem pretty good at taking care of things."

He pulled her back around. "I am good at my job. But I'm still not so sure I can trust *you*. Now you decide these goons are after me, too, or maybe just me, because my name was in your sister's notes?"

Her eyes went cold with dread. "You have to trust me and I have to trust you. You were my last hope. A desperate measure. I was afraid to tell you any of this, but I just now connected on your name as a possible reason for *them* to follow me. But if you don't want to do this, I'll find someone else. Or I'll do it on my own, as I've said. But I will not give up. You didn't. Why should I?"

Hunter wanted to send her on her way and wash his hands of this whole mess. His gut told him that would be a fatal mistake for both of them. Now he was even more involved. If Laura had planned to contact him, she either wanted to hire him or warn him. He'd never know which for sure.

So instead of putting her back on a plane to Oklahoma, he said something that went against every fiber of his being and made him feel sick to his stomach. "Here's the deal, Chloe. I did agree to take on your case and so you'll pay me big bucks and I'll find out what really happened to Laura and I'll find out who's trying to kill you. I'll even find out why these people would want me dead if that's the case."

He moved toward her and cringed when Chloe shrank back. "But I won't be doing it for the Conrads or for you or for any kind of balance. I'll be doing it for Beth. Because she had all the good in her. Too much good for the likes of Tray Conrad." He stopped, held his fist tightly against his jeans. "And I promised my sister I'd always do right."

Chloe stared him down once she got over her initial fear, her expression softening with understanding and then hardening again with grit. He'd give her points for that, at least.

Then she surprised him by reaching out her hand to him. "It's been a long day, but I think we've finally reached an understanding. So let's quit bickering and second-guessing each other and get on with ending this thing once and for all. And I don't care who I have to send to jail. Someone is going to pay for killing my sister."

Hunter took her hand and shook on it, the feeling of her palm pressed against his both killing him and healing him. He thought he hated all the Conrads, but when he glanced down at this one, he didn't have the heart to hate her. She'd lost a sister, too. And she was the daughter of Wayne Conrad's second wife, a younger one who he'd had two daughters with. Chloe hadn't killed his sister Beth. Tray Conrad had done that without anyone's help. And his powerful father had tried to cover up the whole thing.

This confused, determined woman hadn't been

around. Was it really fair of him to blame her for something beyond her control? Or to question her motives for tracking him down?

He told himself that while the lingering scent of her perfume wrapped around him like a wisteria vine and held him in a sweet, enticing vise that wouldn't let go.

And even while he fought against this whole thing tooth and nail, in his heart he knew his time of waiting for some sort of sign that his life was about to change was now officially over.

Pastor Rory always said that God put certain people in your life to make you uncomfortable. Until you figured out why they were there. And once you figured it out, they usually were there for a reason. Such as making you see your own flaws or making you change your views on life. Or…saving you from yourself through grace and salvation.

Did he deserve any grace or any kind of salvation?

Hunter reckoned God was in the details on most things. Especially that "waiting" feeling he'd had since he left Oklahoma. Did God want him to finally let go of his bitterness? Had God sent this woman to him? The stepsister of the drunk who'd killed Hunter's older sister in a fiery wreck just outside Oklahoma City? A Conrad, of all people. What were the odds?

Pastor Rory also said there were no coincidences. Hunter needed to stop listening to that irritating preacher.

EIGHT

"Your friend Bridget, why did she keep texting you?"

Chloe looked up from the laptop Hunter had secured for her, a cup of cold coffee sitting next to her on the table in the break room at the Caldwell Canines Training Center.

"She was concerned about me coming here to find you, of course. I'm sure she's trying to check on me."

They'd been holed up here for two days without incident but she had been digging into past events at Conrad Oil in order to build a timeline of some sort that might connect anything to Laura's death. Piecing together the details only reminded her that she had one last tidbit to share with Hunter. At the right time.

And in the meantime, Hunter had made sure she was never alone whenever he had to leave.

So far, she'd met Alec's wife, Marla, who'd brought sandwiches and cupcakes; Blain's wife,

Rikki, who'd talked fashion with her and brought her an overnight bag of clothes; and Rory's fiancée, Vanessa, who'd told her about her online vintage site and the girls' home she and Rory were opening next year in Birmingham, Alabama.

Vanessa had also invited her to their wedding, scheduled for the Saturday after Thanksgiving. Hunter was supposed to be there. Chloe immediately felt at home with the tight-knit, friendly group of women who'd assured her she was in the best of hands.

Chloe had been so involved in finding Laura's killer that she'd scared off most of the men she'd dated and her friend list had dwindled down to Bridget and a few other employees. But after meeting the group of people who supported Hunter with an unconditional presence, she longed for something like that. Even if they had all made sure she'd better have Hunter back in time for the wedding.

Hunter had shadowed her at every turn and he'd slept right across the hall while a retired K-9 dog named Boomer guarded her door. This place was more secure than the Pentagon, so they'd used the high-tech laptops to find lots of information on Conrad Oil.

But nothing concrete to officially connect her father's company with the Wind Drift Pass Corporation. What little evidence she had was on her laptop and the backup was in a copied file in a safe-deposit box in Oklahoma City.

Now, she and Hunter were back to business. Just business. So she told him about a couple of items she'd found in some recent news articles she'd pulled up earlier.

"Did Bridget know about any of this?"

"Not all of it. At the time, these events and accidents seemed random. Now I'm not so sure."

Hunter rubbed his chin. "So you found an article regarding an online well that had to shut down because someone messed with some of the valves?"

She nodded. "Yes, you know what we call the Christmas tree, where all the valves come together to regulate the flow?"

He nodded. "Yes, I'm familiar with that very important element of an oil rig. It makes everything downstream work to keep the oil flowing properly. And it would be a good place to sabotage a well."

"Yes," she said. "I never even thought of it as sabotage until now, though. Something messed up along one of the lower-mast valves and I remember Daddy being really angry. He said the workover—overtime cost—would be tremendous."

Hunter tapped notes into his phone. "Those lower valves are manually controlled, so it makes sense someone could tamper with one of them. Opening a valve or shutting one off, either way that's not good."

"So that's something we can add to our concerns," she said. "And not long after that, an employee went missing near that location. Everyone figured he'd quit and just walked away from the oil patch. It happens. But now I'm wondering why no one ever heard anything from him."

Hunter made a note of that, too. "Send me the links to those articles." Then he said, "Tell me a little more about your friend Bridget."

"Why?" Chloe asked, surprised. She'd been on the verge of reporting some of the things she still needed to tell him. Now this abrupt twist halted her.

"Humor me," he retorted. "I have to investigate everyone you're close to."

"Bridget and I have been friends since high school. When we graduated from college, my dad gave both of us jobs at Conrad Oil. After college, I took charge of the ranch and the philanthropic arm of Conrad Oil. Bridget is my assistant now."

"Your assistant?" Hunter made more notes on his phone. "Okay, so she'd naturally check in with you a lot. And she knows where you are and why you're here?"

"Yes, but she's the only person who knows beside us."

"Can you trust her?"

Chloe pulled off her reading glasses and shook her head. This man was suspicious of everyone, but then that probably made him good at his job. "Do *you* ever trust *anyone*, Hunter?"

"I asked you first."

"Yes, I trust her. I told you we've been friends for years. She's my right-hand person and a good friend. I'd be lost without her."

"So you hired your best friend?"

"Yes. Is that so weird? She has a degree in business and she keeps thing in order and organized."

"Why did she text you so many times? And leave voice mails?"

"I told you, she was worried about me. She didn't want me to come here."

"You're right. She is a good assistant. You should have listened to her."

"Yes, she's worried, but she knew my reasons for wanting to find you even if she was concerned. She told me that from everything she'd heard, you were scary and not completely human."

"She's right there."

Chloe smiled at that. "She told me about Roxie."

His eyes went wide, a trace of anger shadowing his expression. "What about Roxie?"

"Bridget found the story online about how

Roxie belonged to Beth and how you took the little poodle after—"

"After Beth died." He lowered his head. "I did. I guess that came out in the trial, too." The brooding darkness made his features look harsh. "Roxie saved me from a lot of bad things."

Chloe could see the anguish in that admission. How much had he suffered after going through the trauma of war and then coming home only to lose his sister?

"She also told me about how you drove Roxie around on your bike in a little doggy seat."

He frowned, surprise making him glance up at her. "Yeah, got a lot of stares and snickers on that. But how did Bridget know that?"

"She also read an article about this place, I think. A local reporter told the whole story and I guess the wires or social media picked it up. Sounds like the kind of feature story Laura would have loved."

She got up and poured out the old coffee. The break room was neat and clean and sterile but workable. She'd met some of the staff members. They didn't seem surprised that she was being harbored in secrecy here. But being here alone with Hunter only reminded her of him as a man. That made it hard to focus on researching old articles. She'd rather pick at his brain and find out what made him tick.

Or just stare at him and get her fill of the man.

"You know, if Laura saw that article she might have figured out that you could help her, the same way I did, so she jotted down your name. Laura always had good instincts about people."

Hunter didn't say anything. He seemed lost in another time and place. He looked embarrassed. She wondered how much of this he might already know. Could he actually be involved in something against her family? Was that why Laura had picked at the fringes of his life so much?

"You did a kind thing," Chloe said, hoping to draw him out some more. "You gave Roxie to a little girl, as a service dog to help with her anxieties. Marla's daughter, Gabby. According to Marla, you still visit with Roxie and take her for rides."

He played with his ink pen, twirling it through his fingers over and over. "The dog was cramping my style. But I do visit her in honor of Beth. Roxie was her dog and your stepbrother hated the little ball of fur."

"Tray hated everyone and everything," she said. "But you're different from him. You do have a heart and I've seen it."

"Don't go reading into anything. I'm not wired that way."

"Right." She leaned down over the table and

stared straight into his eyes. "Your secret is safe with me, Hunter."

His deep-ocean eyes skimmed over her. "What secret is that? I have so many."

"This one is the most damaging, I think. Inside that hard shell, you really *are* a nice man."

"Oh, so, you gonna blackmail me on that one?"

"No." She pulled away because being so close to him was more than she was ready for. Knowing about his kind act for his friend's stepdaughter only made him more of a hero in Chloe's eyes. But the way he looked at her, as if he could easily see through her soul, that scared Chloe.

"Let's get back to Bridget," he said. "Did you check all those messages?"

"Yes. She was worried about me not checking in and then she reported a few things that were taking place back at the office." Then Chloe frowned and pursed her lips. "But there were two more that I didn't get to hear before someone dropped my phone on the floor and left it there."

"Sorry about that. Necessary."

He got up and roamed around like a big cat, checking windows and doors, searching the training yard. "We can't stay here forever. As soon as Blain gives us the all clear, we can be on the move again."

"Good. Because I don't want to put anyone else in danger."

"Most of these people are retired law enforcement or they've worked with animals for a long time. Tough and reliable."

"That's reassuring, but with me on the premises, they can still get injured or killed."

"We're on it."

Chloe studied him, taking in his rigid stance and alert, active eyes. The man never let go and he never backed down.

"So we have Bridget, who knows everything about your mission here, and we have your father, who supposedly doesn't know where you are. Anybody else? Does Gerald Howard know you're here?"

"I didn't tell him I was coming here."

"But he knew you were researching me."

"I told him I might hire you for standard operations. Background checks, employee histories, things such as that."

"And he fell for that."

"He didn't argue with me or question me. But we discussed you weeks ago and I've never mentioned my concerns regarding Laura's death to him. I tried to make sure no one knew I was coming here, but I had to tell Bridget so she could field questions for me. I thought I'd covered all my bases."

Hunter kept taking notes. "Howard is the kind

who'd question anything. He's probably been watching you."

"He's not around me all the time and besides, he likes you. He probably would have been the first one to agree with me, if I'd told him the truth."

"Still, everyone is a suspect."

"So you have Bridget, my father and Gerald Howard at the top of the list?"

Hunter finally sank down on a chair and started tapping his fingers on the table. "Yes. Before we dash off to Oklahoma, I'm trying to gather all the facts. We don't have anything solid, but the information you found today could help us there. If your father does own that secret corporation, he's hidden it very well and your missing employee might have stumbled on something regarding that."

"I think Laura did, too. She must have talked to the missing employee. The files she'd scanned showed some pretty solid evidence that Wind Drift Pass is owned by Conrad Oil. She went to a lot of trouble to find something that is such a big secret."

"Someone didn't want her to find it."

"And that's why someone killed her," Chloe added, wanting to ask him so many more questions. Wanting to find out what he might know, if anything. "If I can get to that safe-deposit box and get the other copies, I might be able to find something more there."

Hunter's phone rang and he got up again. Which gave Chloe another chance to watch him. She'd never known a man like Hunter Lawson. He didn't walk. He stalked. He didn't talk. He growled. He didn't smile very much. He frowned a lot.

Her long-distance crush on him had elevated to a too-near awareness that she had not expected. But she couldn't let that get in the way of what they had to do.

Hunter put down his phone and glanced at her. "Blain can't find the two men from the Bay Road incident. But he did give me a message."

"What?"

"Your assistant called the police station when she couldn't reach you. Blain told her he'd look into it, but he didn't tell her you were here. Bridget needs you to call her immediately."

Chloe stood and glanced around. "I don't have a phone, thanks to you."

"You can use mine. It should be fairly secure."

He handed her his cell. "Don't stay on too long."

Chloe nodded, her nerves on edge. Hitting the numbers to Bridget's personal phone, she waited and prayed everything was okay.

Bridget answered on the second ring. "Chloe

I'm so glad you called. Your father knows you went there to find Hunter."

Chloe's gaze crashed with Hunter's. "How did that happen?"

"I don't know. But he's fuming mad and he's on his way to Florida."

"He can't come here. It's not safe," Chloe said. "When did he leave?"

"He planned to get on a plane last night, but I don't think he's left yet. I tried to warn you."

"I know. It's been crazy. I—"

Hunter held up a hand and shook his head. Then he mouthed, *No. Don't tell her anything.*

"I'm okay. I'll explain later," Chloe said. "I have to go."

"Wait," Bridget said. "Chloe, be careful. I...I think someone's been following me. They could be after you, too."

Chloe heart stopped. "Bridget, I'm okay. But you need to watch your back. Don't go anywhere alone, okay?"

"I'll be fine. Just... Things are weird. I have to go."

"Bridget? Bridget?"

Chloe handed the phone back to Hunter. "She ended the call. She thinks someone is following her. I have to go home, Hunter. With you or without you."

"With me," he said. "This is only going to get worse."

"It is worse. My father found out I'm with you and he's supposedly on his way here."

"That's just another pickle we have to deal with," Hunter said, his voice doing the growling thing. "It was only a matter of time, since he's probably heard about Sonny's death by now."

"He could have sent those other people," she replied. "I can't be sure."

"We can't let him get in our way," Hunter said. "We have to move you again."

"I know. But this time I have to go back."

"I'll make arrangements."

He turned and left the room. But not before he checked every window and door first.

Chloe sat and rubbed her forehead, her prayers for Bridget's safety now front and center in her mind. She could handle her father if he showed up here, but she couldn't handle losing Bridget. Not after everything else.

Two hours later, they boarded a private plane provided by Caldwell Industries and were on their way to Oklahoma, darkness and another SUV ahead of them covering their trip from the training center to the small private airfield out from town.

Hunter had half expected them to be ambushed again, but the night was eerily quiet.

"Be safe," Alec said to them before he waved them off. "Remember, Lawson, Preacher is expecting you back in time for his wedding."

Hunter hadn't even thought about the wedding. He'd agreed to be one of the groomsmen. Reluctantly agreed.

"I promised the man," he said. "I'll be there."

Alec took that as fact and stood on the tarmac until the doors of the plane were shut.

"You have friends in high places," Chloe noted, her expression full of admiration for the sleek plane.

"Tell me," Hunter replied. "I'll have to lend Alec my bike for a week to pay back this one."

"Is that a fair trade?" she asked, smiling in spite of her obvious nervousness. She clutched her hands in her lap and kept looking down.

"He thinks so. He covets my motorcycle, but Marla doesn't think he needs one. Too dangerous."

Her head came up. "But not for you."

"I don't have a wife or a child."

And he never would.

Chloe didn't argue with him on that notion. He could tell she was too worried about her friend and her father to think about him and his strange quirks. He was concerned, too.

Blain hadn't found any trace of those hit men, and that bothered both of them.

"You're stepping into something big, Lawson," Blain had told him. "I can only do so much from my end but you need to know these people are like ghosts. They've disappeared."

"But they didn't find us."

"That's because Alec and I went to great lengths to make sure they didn't," Blain said. "But we both know they'll come back, time and time again, until they finish the job."

Hunter appreciated his friend's intervention, but now he was truly on his own. He was about to return to a place that had brought him only misery and heartache. With a woman from a family that had caused his parents shame and humiliation and grief.

I must be crazy, he thought as he stared out at the dark clouds. He'd fought so hard to find some peace and redemption. Now he was back in the thick of it.

But when they landed a few hours later, Hunter found his world had gone from crazy to downright absurd.

Wayne Conrad was waiting for them when they came off the plane. And he had Gerald Howard and two heavily armed guards with him.

NINE

Chloe's gaze met Hunter's before she walked up to her father. She'd been adamant about going straight to Bridget's apartment when they landed, since Bridget wasn't answering calls from his phone. So she probably wouldn't mince words with the man blocking her way.

Hunter took in the deserted tarmac, the sound of a wailing wind only added to the chill moving through his insides. He did not want to be back here and this desolate place only added to the foreboding dread that hit him as hard as that icy wind.

He stayed close to Chloe and waited, every cell in his body on alert.

"Daddy, what are you doing here?"

Wayne Conrad stood wearing an expensive black wool coat that whipped like vulture wings against the bitter midnight wind. His gray hair didn't move, however. It framed his craggy face like heavy snow covering an impenetrable mountain.

Her father gave her a disapproving once-over. "I could ask you the same thing." Then he whipped his harsh gaze toward Hunter. "I got a call from a detective down in Florida. He told me Sonny Bolton is dead. So I need to know who killed him and I want to know what my daughter is doing with this man."

Hunter saw the hatred in Conrad's eyes and matched it, his pulse burning with awareness and rage. "She hired me," he said, not bothering to explain. "And we don't know who killed Sonny. He said you sent him down there to bring Chloe back."

"Mr. Conrad has no knowledge of any of that," Gerald Howard said, his tone cultured and clipped in the same manner as his thick mane of gray-blond hair. He'd always been a social climber and now he was certainly on the top of the heap. His expensive clothes couldn't hide the wolf, however. He sent Hunter a sharp-edged look of intimidation. "Lawson, why didn't you just stay out of this?"

"Chloe hired me," Hunter repeated without any explanation.

"She should have consulted us first," Howard barked.

Now, why did he seem even more annoyed than her father?

Maybe because he'd let Chloe slip through the chain of command?

"I can talk for myself," Chloe snapped. "Did you send Sonny to make me come home, Daddy?"

"Don't be ridiculous," her father said, his expression smug and stoic. "I just heard about all this today."

Hunter remembered that smug face. Remembered the onyx eyes and the stern countenance and the hollow soul inside the man. Conrad was probably lying. How had he found out their plane would be landing here?

"Sonny said you sent him. He was going to tell us more, but someone put a bullet in his chest. We thought you might know about that already."

"Lawson, it's been a while," Wayne Conrad said, his eyes still on his daughter. "But I don't owe you any explanations."

"Then you won't get anything out of me."

"I'm here for my daughter. You can leave now."

Hunter stepped closer to Chloe. He had a sudden urge to grab her and put her back on that plane. Followed by a deep urge to wipe the smug right off her father's face.

But the warning in Chloe's eyes stopped him from grabbing her up and kidnapping her. They'd just shoot him and ask her questions later.

"I see you still travel with your minions," he quipped, nodding toward the guards standing back in the shadows. Gerald Howard kept holding up his hand to keep them in check.

"And I see you still have a smart mouth," Conrad retorted. "But as I said, I'm only here to bring my misguided daughter home."

"I'm not going with you," Chloe said. "Hunter and I have some business to take care of, Daddy. You made a trip out here for nothing. And you sent Sonny down to Florida for nothing. He's dead now."

Hunter had to hand it to Wayne Conrad. His expression went slack as shock filled his eyes. "What are you talking about? I just heard about Sonny being killed and I'm devastated. I didn't send him anywhere. Sonny wasn't the kind to do something like this. I didn't send him, but I'd sure like to know who did."

Chloe gave Hunter a quick glance and then stared over at her father. "He showed up and told me you'd sent him to bring me home. Then someone shot him. Don't try to hide the truth."

"I'm not hiding anything," Conrad said. "I haven't heard from Sonny in days, so I was shocked to get that call from the detective. I even mentioned to Gerald that Sonny must be somewhere on a binger. You know how he was."

Howard stepped forward. Hunter had forgotten

how scrawny the slick lawyer was underneath all his fancy suits. "Your daddy has been worried sick about you, Chloe. When I found out where you were, I told him immediately."

Hunter snorted. "Oh, so you sorted this out. And ran straight to the old man. Figures."

Wayne Conrad shook his head. "It doesn't matter how I found out, but I have no idea why you went all the way to Florida to mess with this man, Chloe. You know his history."

"I didn't know I had a history," Hunter said. "I mean, you tried so hard to wipe my family off the face of the earth, I'm surprised there's any trace left."

"You did that all on your own," Conrad replied. Then dismissing Hunter with a scowl, he turned to Chloe. "Now stop wasting my time. It's turning cold and I want to get home and have a brandy by the fire. But I want my daughter with me." His scowl darkened. "We have to figure out this mess."

"She said she's not going," Hunter retorted, glancing from Conrad to the two goons with the big guns.

The guns came up, aimed at him.

Gerald Howard's condescending grin made Hunter want to punch something. But that wouldn't win him any points.

"And I said she's coming home with me." Conrad motioned to Chloe. "Come on, Chloe. Don't make me have to shoot him."

Chloe's gaze zoomed from Hunter to her father. "Daddy, I need to finish what I've started and I know you won't shoot Hunter. Why would you?"

"I can think of several reasons," her father said, his cold gaze cutting to Hunter. "Right, Lawson?"

"Get in line, Mr. Conrad," Hunter said. "I have a way that just makes people want to get rid of me."

"That mouth is what irritates me," Conrad said. "Always so sure of yourself. You should have stayed in Florida."

"It is warmer there." Hunter nodded toward Chloe. "But your daughter hired me to help her, and as you know, I always finish what I start."

Conrad's rage showed in the deep wrinkles haloed by the airport lights. "Why, you—"

"Daddy, this is my business," Chloe said, moving closer to Hunter. "Go home and we'll talk soon."

"No, you need to come home with me. I've talked to Bridget and she told me the truth. It's over."

Chloe stepped forward and Hunter tried to move with her, but the guns lifted another inch. Toward his head.

"What have you done to Bridget?" Chloe

asked. "She's not a part of this. You can't blame her. What did you do, Daddy?"

"Nothing. She's fine," Conrad replied. "But... she's a bit shaken about you running off on some whim."

"This is not a whim," Chloe said. "Why don't you tell me what you know?"

"I don't know anything," her father said, his hawkeyed stare aiming on Hunter. "Let's go home and we'll talk about all of it. In private. You can call Bridget while I try to get this under control."

Gerald Howard mimicked his boss. "We'll take it from here, Lawson. Go back South before you regret this."

Hunter didn't like that veiled threat. Surely this man wouldn't hold his daughter's assistant hostage. Or his daughter, for that matter. But then, Hunter knew the Conrad way. Anything was possible.

"I'm not going with you!" Chloe marched over to Hunter and grabbed him by the waist and positioned herself as close to him as possible. "I'm going with *him*."

The guns looked confused now. Hunter put one arm around her back and the other in front, across her shoulders and dared them to shoot. Then he placed her behind him, praying they wouldn't try anything.

"Did y'all get that?" he asked, his own weapon hiding under his jacket and pressed against his rib cage. "She's okay. I'll take care of her. But she is not leaving here without me."

Conrad held up one finger and the men lowered their weapons.

"Sir, you don't have to listen to that kind of trash talk," Gerald said, his dark eyes raking over Hunter with disdain.

"I can't shoot my *only* living child," Wayne Conrad said, the emphasis clear. "And I won't shoot you, Lawson, because you're not worth the trouble. But that's mighty tempting. Just know this. I have people everywhere. And sooner or later, she'll come home where she belongs."

He gave Chloe one last fatherly glare. "Your grief has done this. You need to let it all go. Your sister isn't coming back, and if you keep this up, I might lose you, too."

Chloe inhaled a shaking breath, but she didn't speak.

"This isn't over, Lawson. Remember that."

They watched Conrad get into a big black sedan, his bodyguards making sure he was all tucked in and comfortable while Gerald Howard stood glaring at Hunter.

His old friend had completely gone to the dark side.

"They're gone for now," Hunter said, his hand

on Chloe's arm while he still held her behind him. "But they'll be back."

Wayne Conrad's parting comment had held some bite. This was just beginning.

His phone rang. "Hello?"

A weak female voice echoed out into the night. "I need to speak to Chloe."

Hunter handed the phone to Chloe and leaned close to hear. "I think it's Bridget," he whispered.

Chloe grabbed the phone. "Bridget, where are you?"

"At the Conrad cabin. Hurry, please."

The connection ended.

"Something's wrong," Chloe said. "She didn't sound good. We have to hurry."

"Let's get a car and you can show me the way," Hunter retorted, taking her hand.

Chloe pointed to the single-lane road. "Turn here."

"You live out here?" Hunter asked, thinking this cabin she kept talking about was too exposed and too isolated.

"Not all the time," Chloe said. "I live in town in an apartment, but I come out here a lot. Bridget does, too. If she's here we have to find her."

"It's not safe."

"It has an alarm system and I know how to use a gun."

"You don't have a gun."

"I do inside there," she said. "I hope Bridget has it right now."

Thinking she was too reckless after that confrontation with her father and now this, Hunter didn't argue. He had to get her somewhere safe, but right now he understood her friend could be in danger. The woman on the phone sounded frightened and weak. This smacked of something that the Conrads would try to pull, but Hunter had to admit he was shocked that Wayne Conrad would be so vindictive. Plus, the old man had seemed genuinely worried about his man Sonny.

He eased the rental car up to the small cabin. "Stay in the car until I call all clear."

Chloe didn't stay. She got out and followed him while he checked the stark, empty yard out front, his gun drawn. He didn't say anything, but he kept her behind him. Then he checked the front door and saw a tiny yellow light blinking underneath a surveillance camera located on the porch.

"The light's supposed to be red," she said from behind him. "Someone's messed with the alarm."

"I told you to let me check it out first," he retorted. "Go get back in the car."

Chloe rushed past him and started beating on the door. "Bridget, it's me. Let me in."

The door was locked and intact, but something didn't feel right. The night was cold and windy a shutter flapping against the barn he'd noticed out back when they drove up.

"Chloe, listen to me. This could be a setup."

"I have to find her."

"Do you have a key?"

"There's a spare in the wood box." She hurried to a big trunk set underneath one of the windows and found a corner under the lid. "Here."

Hunter took the key, his instincts telling him they should get out of here. But he couldn't leave her friend behind, so he opened the door and tried to keep Chloe shielded.

But she rushed in and switched on lights. "Bridget?"

The alarm code had been disarmed. Maybe Bridget had forgotten to reset it, but he doubted that.

"Chloe, wait."

Chloe ignored him and kept moving, which forced him to move with her while he tried to become acclimated to the layout.

A large den and kitchen with big, chunky furniture. "No one here."

He called out. "Bridget Winston? Are you here?" Nothing.

Chloe pointed to the back. "A bedroom and bath."

He kept her behind him and cleared both rooms.

"There's a loft room where I usually stay," she

said, her gaze moving over the cozy cabin. "She could be up there."

Hunter went ahead of her up the wide-planked staircase.

"Bridget?"

Her friend wasn't in either of the loft rooms.

"What happened to her?" Chloe asked, spinning, her hands in the air. "She said she'd be here. Try her phone again."

Hunter did that, but they didn't get Bridget and they couldn't hear the phone ringing.

Hunter grabbed her hands and steered her away from the log railing that offered a view of the room below. "Chloe, listen to me. Someone is messing with your head. I don't think your friend's been here. But I do think someone lured us here."

"No, it was Bridget. They made her do it and now she might be somewhere hurt or worse."

A bullet pierced the floor-to-ceiling window across from the railing.

Hunter pushed Chloe down and held his body over hers while bullets spewed all around them.

TEN

Chloe held her hands over her head and willed herself to stay down. Hunter covered her like a metal shield, the warmth of his arms around her giving her the strength to stay calm.

When the shooting finally died down, the house went still.

"Are you okay?" he asked, his breath tickling against her neck.

Chloe could feel his heartbeat pounding as fast and hard as her own. What kind of nightmare had she brought him into?

"Chloe, talk to me."

"I'm fine," she said, her voice low and gravelly. "Are they gone?"

"I'm about to find out." He lifted himself up and helped her to a sitting position. "I need you to stay here. I mean it, Chloe. Get in the closet and don't move until you hear my voice."

The thought of him going out there alone terrified her. "What if you don't come back?"

"I'll be back," he said. "We might be outnumbered, but I know a thing or two about sneaking in and out of buildings. If I'm worried about you, I'll be distracted. Promise me you'll stay in the closet so I won't have to worry."

"Okay, I promise." She prayed she'd have the courage to do as he asked. Right now she wanted to scream until she couldn't scream anymore.

"Where is the gun you keep here?" he asked, his voice gentle.

"Downstairs in a safe box in the coat closet."

"We don't have time to get it right now."

She nodded and glanced around. "I'll find something else." When she spotted a heavy brass foot-high sculpture of a deer with jagged antlers, she grabbed it and crawled toward the closet. "I used to have pretty good aim when I played softball."

Hunter smiled, but his eyes held a trace of worry. "Good. But you can't throw that like a softball. Although that thing could really damage something or somebody if you jab it at them."

She inhaled a breath. "I sure hope so."

He helped her to the long narrow closet where old clothes and boots were stored.

"Most of these clothes belong to Laura and me," she told him, a piercing pain hitting her heart. "I haven't had the stomach to give her stuff away."

"That's okay," Hunter said in a hurried whisper. "These heavy sweaters and coats will protect you." He pushed at her long bangs. "Stay put, you hear?"

Bobbing her head, she found a spot behind some blankets and held the shining deer in front of her, antlers first. Then she nodded to Hunter. "I'm good. Go ahead."

He stood and crept out of the room and then she was alone in the silent, still house.

She prayed Hunter would be okay and that Bridget was safe. But where was Bridget? She'd called from here and now no sign of her. The shooters could have taken her...or worse.

Chloe sat there in the dark, thinking about how her life had changed in the last couple of days. Had she brought this on Hunter? Or were these criminals out to get both of them?

Her father had been so angry at the airport, but he acted as if he didn't know about Sonny showing up in Florida. Someone had tipped him off about her, however, but Chloe couldn't see Bridget doing that. Bridget was loyal to her and she'd promised to keep Chloe's whereabouts a secret. But if Chloe's father had forced the issue or threatened Bridget, she might have reluctantly given in and she could have been the one who sent Sonny.

Chloe listened, her breathing loud in her own

ears while her doubts and questions only increased with each heartbeat. Did she hear footsteps coming up the stairs? Or was that her pulse making that thumping sound?

Scooting back against the blankets, Chloe felt something on the old wooden floor. A small bump of an object pressed against the back of her jeans leg, just under her right thigh. Thinking about spiders and other creepy things, she ventured a hand across the plastic and metal object and tugged it out. Only an old tube of lipstick. Absently dropping it into her jacket pocket, she moved closer to the closet door.

And saw a shadow falling across the loft room.

Hunter lay in the dark near the pond behind the barn. From what he could tell, the shooters had left in a hurry. Either someone had scared them away or they'd been ordered to leave.

Since Wayne Conrad had given him a murderous glare with that parting shot at the airport, he could only guess the man had sent enforcers to do some damage. But the man couldn't be corrupt enough to shoot his own daughter without a qualm.

This didn't make sense. Hunter had been trained to take no prisoners, so he knew how hit men worked. They didn't shoot up a place and just up and leave. They'd have to end it with the job complete. Leave no one alive. Yet these people only went so far and then disappeared.

He thought back over the first time they'd come at Chloe at the Hog Wash. One shooter and one bullet from a silenced gun. Then they'd left. And returned, but Hunter had gotten her away before they even pulled off a shot.

Then poor Sonny had been sent on a fool's errand to bring her home. The man didn't even have the gumption to shoot anyone, but he'd been killed straightaway. Why would her father have his own man taken out and then claim he didn't know a thing about it?

And the tire shot out on the Bay Road? Maybe another scare tactic, but then Hunter had fought back and the shooters had either taken off on foot or decided to swim with the sharks.

It was all beginning to make sense now.

Someone was trying to scare Chloe, not kill her.

For now.

How long would they keep coming before they took things all the way? If they didn't want Chloe dead, then maybe they needed to keep her alive for a reason?

They were watching her to see if she had found out the truth. They'd taken her laptop for that reason.

But maybe they hadn't found anything there.

So now they were back, either trying to scare her into stopping her investigation or hoping to jar something out of her.

Once they had the damaging information, they'd destroy both it and her. They'd end it once and for all because she could lead the authorities to the incriminating evidence that would finger someone as the mastermind behind her sister's death. He wondered if that was what had happened to her sister, Laura. If Laura had found evidence they wanted buried forever, they could have gone after her in hopes of getting that evidence. But they'd killed her. A plane crash could have hidden the evidence easily.

Until Laura's sister started the whole thing up again.

He believed that now.

They'd killed Laura before they found what they were looking for, hoping it was over. Had she hidden that evidence, knowing her devoted sister would go looking?

If she had, there might not be an easy end to this. It would be a bad ending unless Hunter could stop it.

Hunter searched the yard in front of and behind the cabin, one step at a time, and promised himself he wouldn't let that bad end happen to Chloe.

He crawled along the cold ground until he was sure no one was lurking around the barn or near the house. No vehicles that he could tell. The long, flat road and the entire pasture down to the pond were both empty.

Hunter decided to check the barn. It would be easy for someone to hide in there. The big doors stood open, but the cloudy, cold night covered the inside of the building with bulging shadows and jagged images.

He moved against the stalls, keeping to the shadows, his gun lifted in a protective stance.

No horses or humans. Just empty stalls and old farm equipment.

He had turned to go back the way he'd come when he heard a noise in a far corner. Almost like a cat meowing.

Hunter whirled and listened. There it was again. A soft moan. He took off running toward the noise.

"Hello?"

"Help."

Weak but definitely female.

Scrambling to move several crates and buckets, he saw a dark form huddled against some blankets. A young, redheaded woman lay curled up on the dirty blankets, blood covering her face.

"Bridget?"

The woman moaned again. "Chloe?"

"She's safe," Hunter said, touching a hand to her pulse.

Weak and erratic. "Bridget, I'm Hunter Lawson. Who did this to you?"

She shook her head. "Chloe. Help Chloe. After…" Her voice trailed off into a moan of pain.

Hunter checked her over for broken bones. When he touched on her ribs, she cried out. Probably cracked.

"I'm going to move you to the house," he said, not sure he could trust anyone to come and help her. He needed to get back to Chloe, either way. "I'll try not to hurt you."

She nodded and passed out.

Chloe didn't dare breathe. She knew the hulking form just outside the closet door wasn't Hunter. He would have called out. The man moved around the loft, the faint light from downstairs casting him in long, grotesque silhouettes as he searched the cabinets and dressers. What was he looking for?

Chloe held her weapon tight, her sweaty hands making the dusty brass figurine warm and sticky. She should rush the big man and stab him with one of these artistic antlers, but he'd shoot her before she ever got in a good jab.

So she sat and prayed that the man wouldn't open this closet door. Then she got practical and did a hurried crawl until she could stand in a corner right by the door. She'd hit him in the head before he could get in a good shot.

The man moved closer. Close enough that she got a good look at his face through the shutter slats. Craggy and pockmarked skin, big black eyes and inky-black spiky hair. He looked familiar, but she couldn't be sure if he was one of the men who'd tried to shoot her in Florida. He moved toward the door, his footsteps so steady and sure she could match them to her own heartbeat.

Placing his hand on the doorknob, he stood still as if expecting something or someone. Another heartbeat passed. Two. Three.

The door creaked open. Chloe could see his hand, big and meaty and full of bulging veins. She had to do this now or he'd kill her.

Taking a breath, she lifted the brass buck, the spindly antlers shining in the muted light. The door flew open and the man loomed over her. Chloe held her scream inside her throat and rammed the object high enough to pierce his face with one of the sharp little antlers. Then she lifted the object again and rammed the brittle antlers against his stomach.

He cried out and grabbed his bleeding face. Chloe lifted the sleek rendition of a majestic eight-point buck and crashed it down on the man's head. He fell forward, grasping for her leg. But she jumped out of the way and screamed.

And because she wanted to be sure the man didn't do anything else, she leaned over him and hit him on the head again, this time using the heavy base of the figurine. She might not be able to knock him out, but she could disable him enough to escape.

"Chloe?" Hunter came bounding into the room with his gun drawn and found her standing over the unconscious man, her hands to her mouth.

She looked from the man to Hunter, her breath shallow, shock weakening her bravado. "I think I killed him."

ELEVEN

Hunter bent down and touched a hand to the man's neck. "He's still alive, but I give you points for trying."

Chloe took in air and exhaled slowly. "Let's tie him up."

Hunter admired her courage, but he had to tell her about Bridget. "I'll take care of him, but right now we have another problem."

Chloe's gaze locked with his, dread darkening her eyes. "What?"

Hunter grabbed a belt dangling on a hook and flipped the man over. Soon, he had the unconscious man's hands bound with the old belt. After checking for other weapons and any information he could find, he dragged the man to the spindled railing overlooking the room below so he could hear him if he made a move.

"Nothing on him to ID anyone," he said on a disgusted breath.

"Okay, now tell me what's going on," Chloe said.

Hunter moved her away from the unconscious man. "Let's go downstairs."

She followed him, her eyes wide. "Hunter, you're scaring me. What's going on now?"

Hunter didn't speak. Instead her took her by the hand and hurried her to the back bedroom. "I found Bridget out in the barn," he said, motioning toward the bed.

Chloe gasped and broke free and headed to the bedroom. "Bridget?" Falling down on the bed, she touched a hand to Bridget's bloody face before glancing back at Hunter. "Is she going to make it?"

Hunter wouldn't mince words. Bridget's short red hair was matted and dirty and she had cuts and bruises all over her face and hands. "I don't know. She's been beaten pretty badly. Cracked ribs and a head wound that I can tell. Probably worse that I can't see."

"We need to get her to the hospital," Chloe said, standing to face him. "Hunter, do you hear me?"

"I hear," he said on an inhale of breath. "I'm pretty sure she has a concussion, but, Chloe, it's risky to leave right now."

"I can't let her die!" Chloe said, tears brimming in her eyes. "She was trying to protect me. We have to help her."

"I understand," he said, putting his hands on

her arms to calm her. "But this man came for you while I was out there. They didn't get what they needed from Bridget, so they came back for us. Or they made her call you to lure you here and then they tried to kill her. And you, too."

"So in order to save me, we let her suffer." She whirled and went to the closet near the door. "No. I'll take my gun and I'll take my chances. Bridget needs medical attention."

Hunter watched as she keyed in the code to the lock box and pulled out an impressive-looking handgun. With expert precision, she unlocked the safety and checked the magazine. "I'm not going anywhere else without this," she said. "Get Bridget some help."

Hunter knew she was fed up, but he didn't like the lethal glare in her pretty eyes. She just might turn that gun on him.

Finally, he nodded. "Okay. Here's what we're going to do. I'll call 911 and report this. The locals will come and cart this man away and get both him and Bridget some help. But I'm warning you, it's going to expose you and everyone will know you're back in Oklahoma."

"They've known that since our plane landed, so what's new?" she asked while she jammed her gun into her purse.

She was right. It was time to face this thing head-on. Hunter stewed for a couple of moments and then made a decision she wouldn't like, but it might be the only way to get to the bottom of things. But he wasn't about to tell her what he had planned. She'd run right out the door.

"You don't make a move without me. These people aren't going to let up."

"I don't care," she said. "I hope they do come back for me. I want this over and done with because obviously I've been right all along. Someone deliberately killed my sister."

"Yes, you're right," Hunter replied. "But I don't want the same thing to happen to you."

"It won't," she said, her eyes meeting his. "I have you with me now."

Hunter wasn't sure she should put so much confidence in him, but he did intend to do his best to keep her alive.

I'll make the calls," he said.

He turned and called 911 and explained the scenario. He really wanted to question the man upstairs before the authorities arrived, so he handed the phone to Chloe. "Stay on the line with the dispatcher while I check on the other injured party."

She took the phone, one hand on Bridget's arm.

Hunter took the stairs two at a time but stopped short when he hit the landing. The belt he'd used was on the floor and the man was gone. Hunter glanced around the room and noticed a sliding glass door he'd missed before.

It was standing open, the cold night air moving over the curtains that had covered it.

Too late to get any answers from that one now.

He checked the room and then went out onto the narrow ledge that had steps down to the back of the yard near the pond. The man had left without a sound.

Another disappearing act.

And still no clue about who was behind all this.

An hour later, Hunter watched the ambulance take away Bridget Winston. She was badly beaten but alive. The EMTs explained that she had a slight concussion and some damaged ribs, plus several cuts and lacerations.

"Let's go," Chloe said, her purse in her hand, her tone impatient and full of a brittle anger.

"Where?" he asked, his mind still on how the locals had been so cool and curt with him. He'd given them the belt he'd used to tie the man, hoping they'd check it for DNA or fingerprints. They wouldn't cooperate with him on this, he had no doubt. Probably threw the belt in the dirt after they got down the road.

"To the hospital," she said. "I have to check on Bridget."

"It's not safe," he reminded her. "Even Sheriff Dickson agreed you needed to find a safe place and stay there. *I'll* go check on Bridget."

The sheriff had finally believed their story— that they'd had a call from Bridget and when they arrived at the cabin, they'd been shot at. But he only gave in and let them off with a statement and a promise to alert him on all accounts after he'd called Wayne Conrad to verify their reasons for being there. Then the sheriff reported back. "Mr. Conrad wants you home, Miss Chloe. He says the ranch is the safest place for you right now."

Chloe had balked at that notion in the same way she was balking at Hunter right now. "So I'm supposed to sit here and wait?" she asked, a hand gripping her tumbling curls. "My father will make sure I'm forced to do his bidding if I let you go alone. I'm surprised he didn't order the sheriff to arrest me for my own good. What do you think I should do?"

Hunter didn't want to answer that obvious question. He wasn't used to dealing with women and their emotions or their need to nurture. He tried to avoid emotions on all levels. If he told her he agreed with her father, she'd pull out that gun and shoot him or she'd have a royal hissy fit.

What could he say to her now?

"You can't stay here," he finally said.

Chloe leaned against the porch railing, her gaze focused on the disappearing ambulance.

Hunter saw the panic in her eyes. "Are you all right?"

"I'm fine," she replied. "I want to talk to the doctors about Bridget. I don't want her mother to worry about her. They're so close."

"What if your father shows up at the hospital?"

"I'll deal with my father." She whirled, all fire and rage. "Take me to see my friend."

"Is that an order?"

"I'm the one paying for your services, so yes."

"I don't like this, Chloe. Going to the hospital is too dangerous."

She headed for their vehicle. "I don't care. I have to make sure she's okay. I'll go without you if I have to."

Hunter took her by her arm and tugged her back. "You need to understand something, Chloe. Bridget's still in danger, too."

She let that sink in. "They wanted her dead, didn't they?"

"I think so," he admitted, not quite ready to tell her his new theory on all this. "But she's still alive and when she's more coherent, I want to talk to her and the locals will want to question her."

"Unless they already know everything," she retorted. "You saw the skeptical expression on Sheriff Dickson's face. He never believed me before and he sure didn't seem to believe me tonight. He thinks I'm ranting about an imagined conspiracy theory."

"He's probably hiding some of the facts regarding this case," Hunter said. "But he has to tread lightly. We don't know who's paying him off, if anyone."

Chloe shook her head. "Right now I'm only concerned about Bridget. I have to go and see her, Hunter. I owe her that much and I don't care if the sheriff or my father shows up. They can't hurt me in a public place." Then she gave him a demanding stare. "And that sheriff had better put a deputy on Bridget's hospital room, too."

"Okay," he finally said. "But I'm sticking close to you, understand? And when I say it's time to leave, we leave."

"Agreed." She brushed past him. "Now let's go."

Hunter checked the yard and hurried her to the rental car. He didn't like the feel of all this. Someone had worked over her redheaded friend and dumped her in the barn like a rag doll. And not only that, they'd left Bridget there and had probably planned for her to be found dead, at that. But Bridget was still alive. They'd want to clear up that big detail.

Then they'd come back to do the same to Chloe. Or at least scare her away.

He couldn't decide what these people really wanted, but something had them on a spree of terror.

He'd given a description of the man they'd injured to the sheriff, but Hunter's gut told him Sheriff Jack Dickson took his orders from a very high up citizen of Conrad, Oklahoma. They'd never hear a thing about that attacker again.

"Get in where it's warm," Hunter said. "I want to check on something."

Chloe got in the car and sat staring out into the night.

Hunter made a quick phone call and then he got behind the wheel.

"What was that all about?" she asked.

"Just clearing up a few things. I'll explain later."

Once they were on their way, Chloe gulped in a breath and dropped her hands into her lap. She didn't speak and he didn't try to talk. Hunter saw things in black and white. There were no gray areas in his mind. He knew what he had to do.

"Somebody is definitely stirred up," he finally said. "At least the sheriff did bring some crime scene people with him, but I'm not sure if they collected any bullet fragments or found any substantial evidence to show who might have assaulted Bridget."

She nodded and wiped at her eyes. "I'm the one

they're after. They didn't have to hurt Bridget." She stared out at the rolling, flat land. "I shouldn't have gotten her involved, but she can be stubborn about things. She kept pestering me until I told her my theory about Laura's death."

Hunter suddenly wished she hadn't divulged that theory to anyone. "Are you gonna be okay if I let you see her?"

"Yes."

Chloe went quiet on him after that. He couldn't blame her. Whoever did this had no morals, and worse, they could make him lose what little morals he had left.

Chloe finally spoke again. "She calls her mom every day. They're so close. Her mom is single. She raised Bridget all on her own."

"Chloe called you a lot, too, while you were in Florida. Are you sure she didn't say anything in her earlier messages that might help us?"

"Not in the ones I heard," she replied.

And he'd disabled her phone in a fit of annoyance before he checked the last two messages from Bridget.

You're slipping, Lawson. Get your head on straight.

Protecting Chloe Conrad had certainly messed with his usual mode of operation. He couldn't miss any more details or they'd both wind up in even worse trouble.

"I'll call her after I see Bridget," Chloe said. "Her mother needs to know what happened."

"No," Hunter said. "You can't make any calls. Too risky. Let the authorities handle that. They probably already have."

"And they'll tell Bridget's mother that she was beat up and left for dead out at the Conrad cabin?" Chloe asked. "I don't think so. Her mother needs to know the truth from me."

"Her mother is probably already on her way to the hospital or she could be there now," he said. "They have to report to the next of kin."

"Fine, then I can talk to her there and tell her how sorry I am that I almost got Bridget killed."

Hunter gritted his teeth. Chloe was going to be very angry with him in a little while. He might as well enjoy the quiet now, while he could.

TWELVE

Chloe didn't want to be here. Hospitals had always scared her with their long hallways and many closed doors. She'd had to identify Laura in the morgue of this same hospital. But she had to see Bridget and make sure she would be okay, so she pushed away the painful memories of her sister's death.

Fear gripped her like two hands strangling the breath right out of her. Afraid her friend wouldn't wake up, she braced herself and wondered what she'd say when Bridget did recover.

If she recovered.

The paramedics had said she was responsive but in and out of consciousness. Chloe had to see her and tell her how sorry she was about getting Bridget involved in her troubles.

Dear God, please don't let anything bad happen to Bridget.

After they parked and Hunter checked the surrounding area, he escorted her inside the main lobby. Chloe waited while Hunter checked in with the front desk, her gaze scanning the long, sterile corridors. Was a killer roaming around in this big place?

When the front doors whished open, Chloe's pulse went into a rapid overdrive. But it was only an orderly returning with a wheelchair. The big open lobby and reception area filled with cold winter air. A storm was definitely coming.

A chill ran over her.

Hunter put his hand on her elbow. "Bridget is still in the ER. But they aren't going to tell us much. You know how privacy laws are, and I can't get past them."

"Did the sheriff send someone to guard her?"

"I don't know. Let's go find out."

He guided her down the hallway to the emergency room area, his hand on her arm, his presence reassuring her that he'd do whatever was needed to keep her from harm.

Chloe thought about the week before she'd finally located Hunter. He'd been a hard man to find and truth told she'd been afraid to face him. Most of her life, she'd heard about the legendary Hunter Lawson. She'd almost given up. She'd prayed for a way out of this, a way to either prove Laura had been murdered or find out that she'd just imagined any wrongdoing.

Seeing Hunter's name in her sister's scrawled

notes had been like spotting a beacon on a dark road. At first, she'd kept finding his name to herself. But finally, she'd told Bridget about how she thought she wanted to find Hunter, just in case he could help her.

Bridget had followed through on what little Gerard Howard had told Chloe, that Hunter had moved to another state. Bridget had verified Hunter *was* in Florida. Bridget had managed to get his address and one of the places he always hung out.

The Hog Wash Rib Joint.

Chloe had been so relieved she'd never asked Bridget how she'd found that last bit of information on Hunter. Maybe Gerard Howard had called Bridget to confirm Hunter's address after Chloe had talked to him.

None of that mattered now, she thought as her boots clicked on the tiled hospital floors. Her prayers were centered on Bridget. Her friend had to recover. Hunter would help her find the truth, no matter what. He believed her now, at least.

Being shot at and chased at every turn could make a believer out of anyone.

They reached the big ER lobby.

"Let's see if we can get some information," Hunter said. He spotted a sheriff's deputy down the hall in front of a curtained room. "Maybe they have Bridget in there."

But when they reached the deputy, the man held up his hand. "Sorry, you can't be here."

Chloe stepped forward. "I'm Chloe Conrad. Bridget Winston is my friend and my assistant and this man is Hunter Lawson. He's with me. I need to see if she's all right."

A woman with short red hair stepped around the curtain, her eyes red-rimmed and misty and an angry frown cloaking her features. "Hello, Chloe."

"Mrs. Winston," Chloe said, glancing toward Hunter before she turned back to the woman. "This is Bridget's mother, Lorene Winston." Then she hurried forward. "I'm so sorry this happened. How is Bridget?"

Hunter went on full alert, his warning gaze moving over Chloe and then back to Bridget's mother. Chloe reached out to the woman who'd been like a second mother to her, noting how much Bridget favored her mother. They both had red hair that they wore short and spiky. Mrs. Winston's eyes weren't hazel like Bridget's. They held more green. But the two looked more like sisters than mother and daughter.

"What do you expect?" Bridget's mother asked, her gold hoop earrings dangling as she pushed away Chloe's outstretched hand. "My daughter is in there in a coma, fighting for her life, and it's all because of you and your shenanigans. I told Bridget this was a bad idea, and I was right."

Hunter's expression filled with shock. "What did Bridget tell you? What was a bad idea?"

"I'm certainly not going to talk to you two about what my daughter and I discuss," Mrs. Winston retorted, turning her back to Hunter.

Chloe was more concerned about Bridget right now.

"But the paramedics thought she'd be okay, that they'd be able to help her here," Chloe said. "What happened?"

Mrs. Winston stepped close to Chloe, but Hunter inched in front of her. "Take it easy."

Bridget's mother glared at him, then waved her hand toward the closed curtain. "She took a turn for the worse in the ambulance on the way here and she's still unconscious. They might have to take her into surgery. She could be bleeding internally."

Chloe felt sick to her stomach. "I can't believe this. I'm so sorry. Can I see her?"

"No. You brought this on her," Mrs. Winston said, her finger jabbing at Chloe. "She adores you and she only wanted what was best for you. You with this crazy notion of going off on some dramatic mission. It's on you if she dies, Chloe."

"Hey," Hunter said, moving between the two women. "That's enough. It's been a long night and we're all tired and worried. But this is not Chloe's fault. Someone is trying to harm Chloe and everyone around her. That's the person who's to blame for this. And if you know anything, you need to tell us."

"Keep her away from my daughter," Mrs. Winston said. "I mean it."

She whirled and headed back behind the heavy beige curtain while the deputy stayed between the curtain and Chloe, his expression daring her to make a move.

"I need to see her," Chloe said, her heart breaking.

The deputy shook his head. "I have my orders."

Chloe turned to Hunter. "Get me out of here."

They headed back to the exit where they'd parked, but before they could leave, the double doors of the main lobby split open.

And Chloe came face-to-face with her father again.

"I've come to take you home," Wayne Conrad said, his tone hushed and fatherly. "This has to end, and I have the means to help." He lifted his head, his chin jutting out. "Let me help, Chloe."

Hunter didn't believe that tone. Not one bit. But he knew in his heart that the safest place for Chloe right now was at home with her father. If Wayne was behind this, Hunter would soon find out. Because he'd struck up a deal with the old man.

"She goes with you only if I go with her."

That was what he'd told Wayne when he called him earlier.

"You want me to come and get my daughter?" Wayne had asked as if he suspected something else.

"Yes," Hunter said. "If you love her, you'll help me protect her. I can't keep fighting these people."

"As long as I allow you into my home, too? You think that will make your job easier? I don't think so. I don't want you in my home, Lawson."

"Look, we're talking about Chloe," Hunter said. "Do you hate me more than you love her? It's your call, man. We'll be at the hospital, but if you try to take her without me, things could get ugly. Think about it."

Hunter now stared down Wayne Conrad, but the older man inclined his chin down a notch. Hunter hoped that meant he'd do the right thing for his daughter's sake.

But Chloe wasn't having any of it. "Daddy, we've had this discussion already. I'm not coming back to the ranch with you."

"Yes, you are," Hunter said, causing her to whirl toward him in confusion. "It's the only solution for now."

"What?" The look of hurt and doubt in her eyes floored him. "What are you talking about?" Then realization and resolve filled her eyes. "Have you been planning this all along, Hunter?"

"No. But I called your dad earlier," Hunter explained, hoping she'd go with it and not make a scene. "We both agree the Conrad Ranch is the safest place for you right now."

"No, absolutely not," she retorted. "I can't believe you'd trick me like this. You know how I feel."

"I only know that someone is after you," Hunter said. "Bridget got hurt and you could be next. They keep trying to scare you right now but sooner or later, they'll make one last move and it might be fatal. You need to be in a secure location."

"And you think my father's home is secure? Hunter, we've talked about this. I can't trust anyone right now."

He took her hand and looked into her eyes. "Do you trust me?"

"I thought I did," she said, her eyes blazing.

"Trust me now, okay?"

She shook her head. "No. If I'm supposed to trust you, then I need to be with you. Not inside the family compound. We agreed."

"You *will* be with him," her father finally said. He sent Hunter a defiant, daring glare. "In my home. He's coming with us. I need to protect you more than I need to go to war with him."

Chloe looked from her father to Hunter. "Is that true?"

Hunter nodded, relief washing over him. "Yes. I told you I'd be with you twenty-four-seven and I meant it. And I told your father if you go home with him, I'm going with you."

"Hunter, are you sure?"

Hunter saw the trepidation in her eyes. Her feelings mirrored the turmoil roaring through his system. He wasn't sure of anything he was doing right now, but this was the only way.

"We can't keep running, Chloe," he said. "The Conrad compound is secure. I can work from there and if I have to follow a lead, you'll come with me or I'll make sure someone I can trust stays with you."

"Along with armed guards," her father said.

Chloe's eyes met Hunter's gaze. She could tell how much this was costing him and it only made her admire him even more. He stared at her with eyes that burned through her soul. She wanted to say so much but instead, she said, "But...you two hate each other."

"I'm trying to keep you alive so we can solve this...problem," Hunter said. "I can deal with the rest as long as I'm able to do my job."

"Come home, honey," Wayne Conrad said, sincerity in his tone now.

Chloe dropped her head and wiped at her eyes. "Only if you two promise me you won't bicker or try to outdo each other. Or kill each other. Because I can't take that right now."

Then she lifted her head and stared at her father, determination in her eyes. "You know, you're a suspect on my list, Daddy. Are you trying to stop me from finding out the truth? Or maybe you're only agreeing to this to lure Hunter back so you can finish him off."

Wayne Conrad's face went pale with shock. "What on earth are you talking about?"

Hunter took her by the arm. "Let's get you home and we'll all have a long talk with your father, okay?"

Chloe bobbed her head and allowed him to guide her out the door. "I'm so tired and I can't fight either of you."

"You can rest," Hunter said, his arm around her waist. "I'll make sure no one bothers you."

He gave Wayne Conrad an intentional glance. "And I mean that."

Chloe couldn't believe what had just happened. She and Hunter were in the back of a black limo, zooming away from the hospital, her father sitting across from them with a stoic expression on his face.

"We need to talk about this," her father said.

Hunter held up his hand. "Not right now, sir."

"You don't get to order me around," Wayne replied. "That was not part of our deal."

Hunter had made a deal with her father. She couldn't imagine how much that had cost him. But her heart got a strange quickening, knowing he'd done this for her.

Hunter didn't seem fazed by her father's admonishments. "I work for Chloe and she's not ready to talk."

"And you know this because?"

"Because he's right," Chloe finally said. "I'm tired and I don't know where to start. You've never wanted to hear me out before."

"But you think I'd try and have my own child murdered?"

The hurt in her father's words tore through Chloe. "I'm confused and suspicious and afraid, Daddy. They wouldn't let me see Bridget and I'm upset about that, too. Someone doesn't want me to know the truth. I'll explain it all later."

Her father stared at her in disbelief. But he didn't question her anymore.

Chloe didn't want to talk to him or Hunter right now. She couldn't stop thinking about Bridget. She missed Laura. She missed her mother. Still shocked by Lorene Winston's reaction to seeing her, Chloe tried to focus on what she had to do rather than how badly she'd failed. She refused to cry, but tears pricked at her eyes and a bone-deep weariness washed over her. She'd figured this wouldn't be easy, but the sheer scope of what had happened over the last few days burned at her like a prairie wind.

"I need to call Mom," she said. "I haven't talked to her since I left. I don't want her to hear any of this, so I'd better get in touch with her soon."

Her father's head came up. "You won't have to call her. She'd coming to Conrad Corners for Thanksgiving. She should be at the house when we arrive."

THIRTEEN

Chloe thought she must have heard wrong. "My mother is coming to your house? Is this a bad dream?"

Wayne Conrad shrugged. "Justine was concerned about you. She said you sounded frantic last time she spoke with you."

Outside, the lights of Oklahoma City sparkled in the distance, reminding her that she was a long way from the tropical breezes of Millbrook Lake.

"I wasn't frantic," Chloe said, shooting Hunter a heated glare for putting her in this predicament. "I was on my way out the door to Florida and I didn't want to get Mom involved."

"Well, she is involved," her father said. "Apparently, Bridget's mother called her and told her everything." He gave Chloe a sympathetic stare. "Lorene Winston blames you for dragging Bridget into your conspiracy theory."

"She shouldn't even know about it," Chloe said. "I don't know why Bridget told her mother any of this. She knows to keep anything we discuss confidential."

Hunter's grunt of frustration echoed over the sleek interior. "Why don't we just hold a press conference and announce this to the world, since rumors are flying left and right? Too many people are aware of this. It's dangerous."

"Her mother has a right to know about this," Wayne said without even glancing at Hunter. "And so do I. I don't like that she went across the country to seek your help instead of confiding in me."

"I don't like that she can't trust you," Hunter retorted.

"I'm right here and I don't like this conversation," Chloe interjected. "Mom doesn't need to rush back here on my account."

Wayne adjusted his black scarf. "Actually, I had already invited her for Thanksgiving before you left on this ridiculous trek."

Chloe couldn't stop the giggle. "You what?"

"Your mother and I have been talking a lot lately," he said, his expression bordering on sentimental. "After we lost Laura, it was awful for all of us, you included, of course. But you know your mother took it very hard. I called her to check on her a couple of times and soon it became a routine thing."

"You and Mom, a routine thing?" Chloe thought

she'd truly fallen down the rabbit hole. But his grief about Laura was sincere and she certainly knew how her mother felt. Laura's death had been tough for all of them, and Chloe had been torn between staying here with her father and moving back to Texas to be closer to her mother.

But she had to protest now on principle because it didn't add up. "I'm glad you were able to help Mom. But you and Mom hate each other."

"That's a strong word," Wayne said. He looked at Hunter. "I know what it feels like to hate someone, and I don't feel that way about your mother. She was my wife for many years and she gave me you and your sister. How could I hate her? We made some bad choices—"

Chloe held up a finger. "*You* made some bad choices."

"Yes, I made some bad choices. But…that's the past. We made our peace after Laura's death. We're pulling together for your sake now."

"That's so sweet of you," Chloe said in a low note of sarcasm, wondering what was really going on. "Bridget's mom is angry at me and I don't blame her, but to call Mom before I ever left for Florida, well, that wasn't necessary at all."

"She wanted someone to know what you were up to," her father retorted. "You wouldn't talk to either of us about this."

"I tried to talk to you," Chloe said. "You wouldn't listen. Nobody would listen."

Her dad held up his hand. "I admit I didn't want to hear it."

"Okay, so I had to find someone to help me."

Her gaze flickered to Hunter. He looked as stoic and silent as always. Probably wishing he could get out of this car and never look back.

How could she have missed Bridget's concern? Yes, Bridget had warned her to think long and hard before going to find Hunter but Chloe assumed that was because Bridget had heard so many rumors regarding Hunter. The man did have a reputation.

But then, her own divorced parents were now cozying up right under her nose and Chloe had somehow neglected to see that. She'd missed Bridget's anxiety even when her friend was trying to talk to her about it. She should have remembered how close Bridget was to her mother, too, and warned her not to mention any of this to Lorene. What else was she missing?

"You know how Lorene Winston can be," Wayne said. "She and Bridget are very close and she hovers. She went into one of her dramatic spins, I'm afraid. I can only image how she must be behaving right now with her daughter in the hospital. Driving the entire staff to distraction. I understand her concerns, of course, but still that woman goes into overdrive sometimes."

"She won't let me see Bridget," Chloe said. "This is more than a dramatic spin. She's worried about her daughter and so am I. It's my fault. She has every right to be upset with me."

"Bridget needed to stay out of it," Wayne said. "I'm worried about her, too, and we'll make sure she gets the best treatment possible. Lorene wants to keep this quiet so the press won't hound them. I agree. The official word is that a guest at our cabin walked in on a home invasion and almost lost her life. But she's asked to remain anonymous."

Hunter sat like a statue, taking it all in. What was he thinking? Was he trying to fit all the pieces of the puzzles together?

Chloe didn't respond to her father, but again, in spite of his official spin on things, she noted humility in him that hadn't been there before. Her father always thought money could cover anything. In this case, she was glad he had the means to help Bridget and that he was willing to understand.

She changed the subject back to her mother. "So, you and Mom? Why haven't you talked to me about this?"

Wayne's face was hidden in moonlight and shadows. "I didn't want to upset you or confuse you. And you've been so preoccupied with this conspiracy theory, I think we lost touch." He shrugged. "It's your way of dealing with your grief."

"No, it's my way of finding out what really happened to cause her plane to crash," Chloe retorted.

"I'm not sorry you're coming home with me," her father said. "But I am sorry you can't move on. It will be good to talk about all this and get it out in the open."

Hunter leaned forward. "Well, now you can catch up. And figure out who's behind this. And then we'll all sit down and have turkey together. A nice little love fest."

"You're not invited," Wayne retorted.

"He's with me," Chloe said. "So that means he gets to eat meals with me. You're invited, Hunter."

Wayne did an eye roll. "We always have plenty. I reckon one more won't change that." He waved his hand toward Hunter. "You can sit at the other end of the table."

Chloe hoped her frown showed the agitation churning inside her stomach. "Can we at least be civil?"

"I can," Hunter said, his tone edged with a sharp dare.

Her dad stared out the window. "I have some

calls to make when we get to the house and then we'll sit down and talk about all this." He gave Chloe an encouraging glance. "I'll try to get through to Lorene Winston, honey. Make her see reason."

"And ask her what she knows," Hunter said.

"I'll do what I can," Wayne retorted before he stalked out of the room. "But I can't see how she knows anything about…whatever you two think you have on anyone."

Hunter grunted again, his eyes on her. "I forgot Thanksgiving is next week. I hope to be gone by then anyway."

Chloe's heart hurt on that thought. He'd do his job and then he'd just disappear back into his self-imposed exile. She'd have to forget Hunter Lawson.

But how would that be possible?

An hour later, Hunter's whole body burned with irritation and anger. He would rather be walking through a minefield than be standing here.

No. Change that. He'd seen enough of death because of minefields to know he shouldn't even think along those lines. But he did not want to be here. Period. End of discussion. Being inside the Conrad compound was a slow torment that stabbed at him like an Oklahoma hailstorm.

And yet here he stood in front of a massive stone fireplace that roared with an expensive fire, a fire fueled by big, fat chunks of sturdy wood that burned in beautiful perfection.

Not anything like the rusty space heater his parents used to have to crank up to stay warm in the harsh Oklahoma winters.

This whole house reeked of opulence and ostentatious excess. Massive and put together with brick and stone and heavy wooden beams, with rambling high-ceilinged rooms and dark-paneled cubbyholes, it looked impressive and overwhelming. A winding, curving staircase twisted around a spacious entry hall and led to a wide balcony that overlooked the first floor. On the second floor, several spacious bedrooms and bathrooms, a game room and a cozy library and den finished out the house. A castle out on the prairie.

But he'd insisted on checking every room for anything that looked suspicious. Now he had to find out where Chloe would be staying so he could be as close to her as possible.

Never had he dreamed he'd be thinking those kinds of thoughts.

Never had he dreamed he'd be standing here.

"I'm glad you're here."

He whirled from the fire and found Chloe staring at him from the wide-open doors to the square den where a maid had deposited him after he cleared the house, two stoic guards trailing behind him. No sign of them now, however.

Just Chloe, silhouetted in front of that curved staircase and looking for all the world as though she belonged here.

"I wouldn't let you come alone," he said, his voice going low and husky.

"You don't want to be here, though," she replied. "That's obvious, of course."

He didn't force an answer. He'd been on the phone with Blain and Alec, telling them what he could. Normally, he didn't share the details of a case, but he wanted this one to go by the book and Blain was a whiz at following the rules even when he broke them. Alec was smart and observant and discreet. He'd help where he could. Plus, he knew people in high places. They'd both agreed to help him with some background details.

Chloe's boots tapped across the hardwood floor. "I ordered coffee and sandwiches."

He wasn't very hungry. "Which is your room?"

That question seemed to throw her, since he'd been through the whole house. "Upstairs. Didn't you check it?"

He'd smelled her perfume in one of the big rooms, but he didn't tell her that. "I checked all of them, but I want to be sure."

"I haven't lived here in years, but it's still available whenever I visit. Second floor. Third door on the right."

"Then I need to be inside the second door on the right."

"You're across the hall in a guest room. My father will put a guard in the hallway."

"Right." He didn't trust that plan, but across the hall might work, since he'd patrol more than he'd sleep.

"Hunter, you said I'd be safe here. Or did you bring me here so you could go back out there without me?"

He stalked close, so close he could see that she'd freshened up and changed into jeans and a big sweater. But the floral scent around her remained the same. "I told you I'm not letting you out of my sight."

"Okay." She seemed to accept that. "Dad will be down in a minute. He got word my mother is on her way."

"Are you all right with that?"

"I'm not sure." She moved around the opulent leather sofa and headed for the fireplace. "For years after the divorce, they didn't speak. Lawyers and assistance-arranged visitation, plane tickets, gifts for birthdays and Christmas. But she always encouraged Laura and me to come here and visit and she seemed okay when Dad offered me a job right out of college. She told me it was my legacy."

"That's a mighty big legacy for anyone," Hunter interjected.

"Yes, it is." Chloe stared into the fire. "Laura balked at working for him, but she loved him. She was here almost as much as me. Our father has always been firm and loving with us, but he never overindulged us. Losing her brought Dad and me closer together…until I started wondering more and more about her death. Even my mother warned me to let it go, but I can't."

Hunter didn't want to admit it, but he said, "I guess even the worst of people have someone they love in their lives. Your mother must still care about the old man."

She held her hands together. "Well, at least they're friends again. That's something interesting."

Hunter felt a rending inside his heart. He knew grief, so he understood how it could take many forms. "Maybe their grief brought them closer together, just the way he said. That can be a blessing."

"Not if he's involved with what happened to Laura. That would devastate my mother."

"Then we need to prove who *is* involved."

"Are you saying you don't think my father is, after all?"

Hunter came to stand by her, his back to the fire. "I'm saying I don't know yet. He's hard to read. Or maybe I can't read him because I just don't want to see him at all."

Chloe gave him a direct stare that made him feel closed-in and vulnerable. "And yet here you are."

He met her gaze and saw the gratitude in her eyes, accepted the need to help her find the truth. And tried to ignore the attraction tugging him toward her. "And yet here I am."

She opened her mouth to say more, but they were interrupted by a ruckus at the front door.

"Where is my baby? Let me see my Chloe."

"That would be my mother," Chloe said, whirling to face the big double doors opening to the entry hall. "Brace yourself. If you think my father is formidable, wait until you meet her."

Hunter grunted again. He had no words for the bizarre twist his life had taken. He should be sitting on a dock somewhere in Florida.

Chloe shot him a wide-eyed warning. "Don't bolt on me now, Hunter."

She was already beginning to know his moods.

And that scared him more than both of her parents put together.

FOURTEEN

Chloe hurried into the hallway. "Mom?"

Justine Conrad glanced up from her stacks of designer luggage and looked into Chloe's eyes. She wore a dark pantsuit and lots of pearls and diamonds. Confident in her own career as a buyer for a large department store, Justine Conrad always looked like a million dollars, as Chloe's dad used to say.

"Darling, you looked exhausted. Have they fed you? Is your room ready? What in the world is going on with you?"

"Slow down, Mother," Chloe said as she walked into her mother's arms. The smell of Justine's classic perfume engulfed Chloe. "I'm okay. Food is being prepared for all of us and my room is ready. So is yours."

She backed away and gave her mother a quizzical stare. "Words I never thought I'd speak in this house."

Mom actually looked sheepish, something

Chloe rarely saw in her beautiful, glamorous mother. "It's a long story, but…well…the holidays are coming and you're in crisis and—"

"I'm not in crisis," Chloe retorted, drawing back more. "I'm okay, Mom."

Justine's big brown eyes searched her face. "I'd say getting shot at and chased and dragged across the country is some kind of crisis. I'm so glad your father convinced you to come here."

"I'm okay," Chloe said, although hearing everything she'd been through from her mother made it sound too real. "I'm in good hands."

Justine looked past her with an appreciative stare. "I should say so."

Chloe turned to find Hunter standing near the doors to the den, his hands in the pockets of his jeans, his expression full of distrust and bemusement. He looked mysterious and dangerous, his features etched in sharp angles and dark shadows. He held all the traits of every bad boy her mother had ever warned her away from. But his saving grace was in the quiet strength that surrounded him like a shield.

"Mother, this is Hunter Lawson. I believe you're familiar with him even if you've never met him."

Justine moved toward Hunter, her hand held out, her diamond rings glittering. "Oh, yes, I

know all about this one." She reached out a hand
and waited while Hunter reluctantly shook it.

"And I know you've hired him to help you with
this mission of yours. I just don't understand why
he's here in your father's home of all places."

"None of us do."

Chloe turned to find her father exiting out of
his office at the back of the first floor.

"I hope someone will explain," her mother
said, her head moving back and forth as she
took in the scene. Chloe knew that look. Her
mother was summing up the situation and probably thinking one of these people looked entirely
out of place here. And certainly thinking that
even though Hunter's being here was confusing
on so many levels, he cut a nice figure standing
in the doorway and, well…he was single.

Justine wasn't one to push the "getting married" issue, because she believed a woman had
to love herself before she could love anyone else,
but she'd always wanted both of her girls to experience "true love."

That wasn't going to be the case here, however.

Hunter was here for a reason and he was being
paid to stay by her side. But once this was over,
he'd be gone in a flash of rubber burning the
road.

"Let's go into the den," Chloe said. "I'll go
check on the food."

"I'll check on the food," her father said. "Get your mother settled and quiet."

"Some things never change," Justine said. "He still thinks I talk too much."

Chloe guided her mother past Hunter and gave him an imploring lift of her eyebrows. She could only guess what was going through his mind.

His phone buzzed. "Excuse me," he said, turning away and heading to a far corner of the den.

"He's…intense," Mom said, a soft smile on her wrinkle-free face. "How are you really, darling?"

Chloe wasn't sure how to answer that. "I'm all right. Shaken and confused and unsure what to do next, but I'm not giving up on this, Mom." She took her mother by the arm. "I know Lorene Winston called you, but you need to tell me what she said. Bridget wasn't supposed to repeat any of this."

Justine shook her head, her symmetrical blond bob floating right back into place around her high cheekbones. "I'm glad Bridget confided in her mother, but Lorene didn't give me the details. She just said it was all too dangerous. Look what happened to the poor girl. Think what they could do to you."

"All the more reason to continue," Chloe retorted. "Why would someone follow me to Florida and try to kill Hunter and me if there isn't something to this?"

She thought about what she knew, a sick feeling roiling inside her stomach. She couldn't withhold anything now. Hunter needed to know all of it.

Her mother considered that for a minute and then glanced at Hunter. "Then let your hunky he-man handle it while you're safe here with us."

"I started it," Chloe said, "and I'm going to see it through. Hunter will be with me at all times, so you can rest assured I'll be safe."

"I'll admit he shouts *formidable* and *capable*, but what if he can't protect you?" Justine asked, whirling when a maid wheeled in a cart with roast beef sandwiches, fruit, crackers and cheese on it. "This is serious, Chloe."

Chloe's father followed and directed the maid to put the cart over by a small table in the corner.

"Let's sit," Chloe suggested. "I'm tired."

"Of course." Mom took over and poured Chloe some water and coffee. "Wayne, come over here and get some food."

Chloe watched her father. He seemed unusually distracted. Normally, he and her mother were politely civil but avoided each other like the plague. Now he didn't even notice her bossy mother demanding him to come and eat. But then, Chloe had caused all of them to become distracted. At least she finally had their attention.

Hunter put away his phone and came over to

the table, a frown creasing his already brooding expression. Her father sat down and pointed toward the chair across from him. "Lawson, take that chair and eat some food."

Mom made a face. "Don't order him around, Wayne. He doesn't work for you."

"Thankfully not," Wayne retorted.

"We can agree on that," Hunter shot back. "My daddy worked for you for years," he said, his gaze raw and harsh. "A roughneck, through and through. Until he had to retire for health reasons." His gaze lifted as he took in the room. "It's rough on a man out in the trenches. He passed away last year. He never was the same after we lost Beth."

The room went still, the very air caught in the net of a heavy grief that seemed to fall over all of them.

Chloe's heart hurt for Hunter. She'd had a good life in spite of the things haunting her now. Even after her parents had divorced, her daddy supported them and her mother worked hard to make her own way, allowing all of Wayne Conrad's money to go to her two girls so they could get good educations but on their own terms.

"I'm sorry to hear that," Justine said, her tone quiet and full of true regret. She sent Chloe a beseeching glance and then stared over at her ex-husband. Wayne Conrad's features had turned to stone.

"I'm sorry, Hunter," Chloe said. "For so many things."

Hunter's curt nod only showed the pain he held inside.

Wayne Conrad looked up but didn't respond. But Chloe caught that trace of regret and anger in her daddy's eyes.

Hunter helped Chloe with her chair and then waited for her mother to sit. Chloe glanced from one to the other. "We agreed to be civil. Since everyone knows why we're here, I thought I'd catch both of you up." She looked from her mom to her dad.

"I'm anxious to hear," Mom said. "I can't believe someone would deliberately hurt Laura and come after you, too."

Chloe and Hunter quickly spelled out the details of the last few days, leaving out the part about what Laura had found about the secretive acreage called Wind Drift Pass. They'd agreed earlier to keep their suspicions regarding her father to themselves for now. If he was up to something illegal, they couldn't very well tip him off that they knew.

Chloe just wasn't sure yet how she'd handle ratting out her own father.

"It seems Laura was onto something that could ruin some very high up people," Chloe said. "We believe someone killed her, hoping to destroy that information. When I became suspicious and started looking into what it could be, they decided to come after me." And Hunter. She couldn't forget that.

"So you don't know what she found?" Mom asked, worry clear in her wide-eyed expression.

Hunter gave Chloe a warning glance. "I think they believe Chloe has the information Laura found and so they're trying to keep this quiet, whatever it is, by intimating Chloe."

He leaned up, his fingers tracing the etched gold on the coffee cup rim. "They could easily have killed us by now, but they keep toying with us instead. They don't just want us. They want the information they think we have. That's keeping us alive."

Chloe and Hunter both watched her father, but he sat perfectly still, surprise coloring his ruddy cheeks, a distant stare settling in his eyes. He was calculating something, but he wasn't going to share it with them right now.

Her mother looked pale and ashen. Worried. Then she looked at Wayne Conrad. "We have to face facts. Someone is after Chloe now and that means she might be right about this after all. Laura might have been murdered, Wayne."

"She *is* onto something, without a doubt," Hunter said. "Not only has she been threatened, but I've been receiving phone calls warning us to back off." He looked her father square in the eye. "And they seem to be coming from a cell tower not far from here."

He studied their expressions to see who didn't look surprised. Wayne Conrad's eyes widened in disbelief. Chloe appeared shocked and afraid. Justine Conrad didn't even blink.

Interesting.

He focused on Justine. "Anyone here care to enlighten me?"

"Are you suggesting one of us knows something about this?" Wayne asked, all bluster and puffed-up pride.

"I'm not suggesting anything," Hunter retorted. "But if one of you knows something about these phone calls to me, you'd better tell the truth now. Because if I find out later you're involved, it won't be pretty."

"You're fascinating," Justine said with a soft smile. "I can see how you finally got to the truth about your sister's death. So I believe you'll find out the truth about Laura's death, too." She glanced at Chloe. "You were wise to hire this one, darling."

Justine Conrad's attempt to deflect the seriousness of this almost made him want to lash out at both of them. Did she know something she didn't want to reveal?

Chloe's father snorted and wiped his hands on a linen napkin. "I wouldn't be so sure about that. You seem to forget what he put this family through a lot."

Hunter wanted to stand and knock over the table, but for Chloe's sake he restrained himself. "Right back at you, old man."

Justine took Wayne's hand. "We're not going to get into that now. We have Chloe to think about. And I think we've found someone who'll be her champion."

"Have you been analyzing me?" Hunter asked Justine so he could get his mind off ringing Wayne Conrad's arrogant neck. And hopefully make both of them see reason.

"Of course." She held her three-strand pearls tightly between her fingers. "After all, you have a reputation around here. Did you think I'd trust you with my daughter's life without having you thoroughly checked out?"

"You did a background check on him?" Chloe asked.

"We both did," Wayne replied, his expression daring either of them to protest.

"I'm twice blessed," Hunter retorted on a droll note. "So, how'd I do?"

"You have an admirable dossier," Justine said, lifting her water glass in a salute. "Heroic, actually."

"I'm glad you approve," Hunter said. "And how about you, Mr. Conrad? Did I pass muster with you?"

"You're still alive and sitting here," Wayne said. "That should tell you something."

Hunter couldn't argue with that. "Who do you think would be making threatening calls to me?"

"What did they say?" Chloe asked, her expression taut with apprehension, her eyes dark with fatigue.

He told them about the first call. "It came right after we hid Chloe at the canine center."

"Tell Chloe Conrad to go back to Oklahoma before she loses everyone she loves."

Chloe gasped. "You never mentioned that to me."

Hunter saw the distrust in her eyes. "You had enough to deal with."

Justine took a sip of water. "Well, she's back in Oklahoma now and you're still getting calls. What did the latest one say?"

Hunter didn't want to alarm anyone, but they had to be diligent. "It said if we don't back off, things will explode all around us and the real truth will come out."

"That sounds like a veiled threat," Wayne said. "I'll bump up security."

"Not just here," Hunter said. "If this is a bomb threat, you have to consider all of your properties."

Chloe stood and held on to her chair. "You mean the well sites, too?"

"Especially the well sites," Hunter replied.

Chloe listened while her father barked orders over the phone and beefed up security around the house. Hunter paced back and forth, his fingers working against his phone screen.

She didn't know who he was texting, but she had a feeling he was calling in some favors to get more information. They already knew of problems at the one site and a missing person whom no one seemed too worried about finding. Maybe this went beyond Laura's death. Someone could be trying to ruin her entire family and the legacy her mother wanted Chloe to have.

She didn't crave the legacy, but she would fight to keep what her father had worked to create.

How could she find out the answers without letting her father know that they still suspected him? Surely he wouldn't sabotage his own operation. And yet all was fair in oil and money.

Chloe didn't like feeling this way about her own father, but Wayne Conrad had a ruthless reputation and a powerful, far-reaching influence. His money could buy just about anything. Especially if he offered it to a struggling roughneck with a family to feed.

A heavy dread filled her soul. She was beginning to think she knew which family her father might have targeted. But she prayed she was wrong.

I have to talk to Hunter and tell him the rest of what I found out. He won't like it and it might be nothing, but I owe him the truth.

Had her father offered Sonny a lot of money to mess with an oil patch or to make that ill-fated trip to Florida? Was he paying someone even as they sat here to scare her and Hunter off the trail? If so, he was playing a dangerous game with her life. With everyone's lives.

Chloe glanced at her father and decided she wouldn't go down that thought path again. Innocent until proven guilty.

She thought about Laura's discoveries. Wind Drift Pass was real, but her father had never mentioned it and she hadn't seen an official memo or file regarding that property. Then again, she didn't work in the contracts and acquisitions department.

Her job was more public relations and making sure Conrad had a nice clean, community-friendly image. That and trying to keep this ranch running took up most of her time. But if Conrad Oil had acquired a new parcel of land, everyone would know about that.

Her father bought up a lot of property and sat on it, waiting for the right time to drill for either oil or gas or to turn it into a subdivision or commercial property. But that was usually public record. This project had gone through so many twists and turns it had been buried like a secret treasure underneath a fake company's masthead.

Why was her father hiding Wind Drift Pass behind a shell company? She wanted to ask him that herself, but then if he was behind all this… She couldn't even think along those lines.

She needed to find out what Hunter was working on and then she'd come clean on everything.

So she stood and glanced at her mother. Justine had gone quiet on her, and that was never a good thing.

"I think I'm going up to bed, Mother," she said, loud enough for Hunter to hear her. "I can't focus anymore. Tomorrow, Hunter and I need to get back to work."

"Of course." Her mother stood and smoothed her suit jacket. She hugged Chloe close and then stood back. "This is like old times, isn't it? All of us gathered here for Thanksgiving…and then Christmas."

A deep sadness swept over Chloe and it was

mirrored in her mother's eyes. "I miss her so much, Mom."

"I do, too, honey. It's going to take some time, but that's why I felt we should all be together this year. Now I'm worried about you. Is this quest really so important that you'd risk your life for it?"

"Isn't it worth knowing what really happened to Laura?" Chloe asked, a lump forming in her throat. "Don't you want to know the truth?"

"It won't bring her back," Justine said, shaking her head.

"But it will bring some sense of justice," Chloe retorted. "I need that in order to…heal."

Justine didn't look convinced. "I don't want to lose you, too."

Chloe glanced at Hunter. He'd put his phone away and was now watching her. "I'll be fine, I promise."

She kissed her mother and nodded to her father.

Wayne gave her a stoic stare and then shifted his gaze toward Hunter.

"I'll walk you to your room," Hunter said, already reading her thoughts.

He thanked her mother for dinner and gave her father a slight nod. Then he followed her out of the den.

"There's a small library on the second floor,"

Chloe said. "It used to be my mother's office and den. We can talk there."

Hunter's eyes moved over her face. "You want to talk?"

"Yes. I need to know what you were doing on your phone after we ate dinner."

"Okay. I'll explain when we're alone."

"Has something else happened, Hunter?"

"Not yet," he said. "But it's gonna be a long night."

FIFTEEN

Chloe guided him into the room centered in the upstairs hallway. The big rectangular room was more light and feminine than the den downstairs, with creamy blue walls and a big bay window that had a stunning view of a lit swimming pool and garden down below. Hunter had checked it for bugs or cameras before, but he could have missed something. So he put a finger to his lips in warning.

"Careful," he said on a whisper. "Someone could be listening."

After shutting the door, she turned to face him. "So, should we just sit and wait?" she asked in a soft returning whisper that tickled at his heightened senses.

Hunter couldn't lie to Chloe. He still had a few friends in Oklahoma and he'd called some of them to do a little checking.

"I've got people watching," he said. "Now that we know about the Wind Drift Pass property, we have to assume something could happen there soon or at least near there. And that cryptic warning I got only verifies that."

"How did you figure out the call was coming from a nearby tower?"

He pulled her to the center of the room, where it would be hard for any listening devices to pick up their conversation. "Another PI I know helped me out. I worked for him before I went down to Florida, and occasionally he calls me in on cases."

"Someone Gerald Howard knows?"

"No," Hunter said, shaking his head. "I don't trust him. He seemed really proud of himself last night."

"He does reek of attitude," Chloe admitted. "He's always been protective of my father and the company."

"I'll keep an eye on him, don't worry."

She nodded and pushed at the golden-brown curls that seemed to always escape and touch on her temples. "So it's probably best if I don't know how you found the information."

She seemed jittery, but then she'd been through a lot. "Probably."

"I'm going to scream if I have to sit around here, Hunter."

"We're not going to sit around. I have a small laptop that Alec gave me when we were leaving.

It's secure and should be safe. I'll get it and we'll see what we can pull up from Conrad Oil. That is, if you have access."

"I have access, but I've already checked our stored online content and the hard copies in the file room. There is nothing about Wind Drift Pass anywhere within Conrad Oil's archives." She stared at the coffee table. "I wish I knew how Laura found out about Wind Drift Pass."

"There's always a way to hide files. Especially these days with the Cloud out there. Who knows what's floating around undiscovered?"

"Which makes our search even that more impossible."

"We just have to fall back on the old-fashioned way of finding information. We hit the streets. And we go out to that land and investigate it."

"I'm all for that, but you brought me to this fortress and now I'm under lock and key."

"We'll use that to our advantage," Hunter said, wishing he could make this easy for her. "We can do a lot of footwork by digging up information online."

She looked skeptical and then said, "Well, let's get started." Then she sat staring off into space, a worried expression on her face.

Hunter nudged her with a touch to her hand. "Think where else your father might have hidden that kind of information. He's more old-school than up-in-the-cloud. A lock box or safe-deposit box, maybe? A locker somewhere?"

Chloe shook her head. "Everything's pretty much electronic now. But we have paper files, of course. I've scoured the file rooms and the backup computer files. I searched maps and titles and land deeds, not to mention real estate transactions and everything else, based on what I think Laura was searching for. The only thing I found was the paperwork about Wind Drift Pass Laura had in *her* files. I have no idea where she got those papers."

"Where are the backup copies you saved?"

"Those are in a safe-deposit box at a bank downtown. No one knows about that."

"Then we'll start by going there first thing to-morrow."

Chloe moved to the big window and stared out into the night. A cold wind howled around the rambling house. "The weather forecast didn't look promising from what I saw on the evening news. Possible snow and ice in the coming week."

"You should rest," Hunter said. "We can't control the weather, but we can keep searching for the truth."

He walked over to stand with her and thought about that howling wind. The sound brought back too many memories of shivering in a ratty old trailer home that sat on a barren, treeless piece of land on the outskirts of Conrad. All red clay dirt and barren emptiness. No hope and no way out. A filth that couldn't be washed away. A stigma that wouldn't give him any redemption. He remembered his daddy working day and night, especially after they'd lost Beth. Gaunt and hollow, dead inside, Bill Lawson did whatever needed to be done to survive.

It had killed him.

"I doubt I'll get any sleep," Chloe retorted, her arms folded against her stomach in a protective stance. She had no idea how much this was costing him, and he'd never tell her.

"Me, either." He glanced around. "This room is between our rooms, right?"

"Yes. One reason I put you in the one across the hall. It makes me feel a little safer with this bridge between us."

They had a lot of bridges between them, Hunter thought. And he needed to remember that each time he looked at her pretty, pouty lips and stared into her golden-brown pecan-shaped eyes.

"Hunter, there's something I need—"

He placed his arm across her shoulder before he'd even realized he'd done it. She glanced up at him, her eyes wide with surprise and something else that he didn't want to consider.

He lifted his hand away and stared out into

the night, the burn of that gesture only reminding him of the burn inside his heart.

"Hunter—"

Before she could say what she wanted to say,
his chin went up. "Did you see that?"

Chloe leaned toward the window and stared
into the night. "I see it."

Hunter saw it again. A flash of light near a
big building out past the yard proper. And it was
growing.

"Fire!" Hunter went into action. "Let's get out
there."

Chloe was right behind him. "I'll call 911 and
alert Daddy. They didn't wait very long to strike,"
she shouted.

"No, and they'll keep striking until they find
what they want."

"I'm going to find my parents."

She started to hurry into the den, but Hunter
grabbed her by the arm. "Be careful, Chloe. Stay
inside unless you have your father and his guards
with you."

She looked up at him with fear in her eyes.
"You need to be careful, too."

He nodded and rushed toward the back of the
house while he shouted into the phone to the 911
dispatcher. By the time he'd run all the way to
the big barn on the edge of a large open field, the

fire had grown and was now shooting up into the cold night sky with an angry, crackling flare.

Their pursuers were growing bolder with each attack.

And Hunter was beginning to think he was far too outnumbered and overpowered to protect Chloe anymore.

"What on earth?"

Justine came out of her room on the other end of the house and rushed down the stairs to meet up with Chloe.

"One of the outbuildings is on fire," Chloe said over her shoulder. "Where's Daddy?"

"He went to his office after I told him goodnight."

Her mother followed her through the house until they'd reached the stately office across from the kitchen and dining room.

"Daddy?"

"Wayne?"

They were both at a frantic pitch now, but Chloe tried to calm down so her mother wouldn't get upset. She stopped at the door of her father's office, afraid of what she'd find. Telling herself to relax she took a deep breath and prayed her family would be all right. And Hunter, too. She asked God to protect the man she'd brought into this.

"He's not in here," she said, turning to grab her mother after she'd checked the office and the adjoining bathroom. "Maybe he heard Hunter calling 911 and went outside."

"The guards aren't anywhere around, either," Justine said.

"Maybe they went out with Daddy." Chloe hoped her father was safe with his men. Exhaustion and fear pulled at her like chains, but adrenaline beat with each pump of her pulse.

She had to go out and find Hunter and her father.

Justine whirled toward the back of the house where a three-car garage graced one side of a large parking area and a matching wing on the other side held a huge media and game room.

The back door stood open.

"Wayne?" Justine wrapped her lush blue robe close after the wind whipped by in angry roar.

"He must have gone to check on the fire," Chloe said. "Stay here, Mother. I'll go look for him."

"Where are the guards?" Justine asked, her neck straining as she stared into the cold night. "You can't go without protection, honey."

"They could be with him."

"Then you don't need to go out there," her mother insisted. "Stay here with me, please. So I'll know you're all right."

Chloe heard the desperation in that plea. Her mother was a strong woman, but she'd already lost one daughter. As much as she wanted to run toward that fire and Hunter, she couldn't leave her mother standing here frightened and alone.

"You're right," she said, reaching to take her mother's arm. "We should stick together."

Her mother heaved a breath of relief. "Thank you, darling. I'll make a pot of coffee."

Chloe couldn't stomach any more coffee right now, but she didn't protest. Let her mother find something to keep her occupied for a few minutes.

Chloe stood in her father's office and watched out the floor-to-ceiling window. The fire was growing with each minute that passed.

Where was the fire truck?

And where was Hunter?

Hunter hurried toward the big industrial building. At least it wasn't all wood. Mostly steel and heavy metal, but no telling what was stored inside that could explode and send shards of shrapnel through the walls and windows.

He stopped a few feet away, the intense heat overpowering and brutal, the acrid smell of choking smoke rising in the wind. When he heard sirens off in the distance, he breathed a sigh of relief.

Until he heard someone calling for help from inside.

"Hello?" Hunter called out, rushing toward one of the open doors. "Who's there?"

"Lawson?"

He knew that voice. "Mr. Conrad?"

"I need help! Hurry."

Hunter only hesitated a moment. What if this was a setup?

"I'm hurt," Wayne Conrad called out. "Please."

Hunter took off his jacket and covered his head and rushed inside the cracking, scorching building. "Call out to me," he shouted, the stench of singed metal and steel making him gag.

Black smoke poured around him in an eerie, liquid fog and cut off his breath and his vision.

"Where are you, Mr. Conrad?"

"I can't see," Wayne shouted. "On the floor. Near the office."

An office. Hunter glanced around. The place was some sort of storage barn. He spotted lawn mowers and tractors, golf carts and maybe a big fishing boat. It was hard to see in the gathering smoke and flames.

But Hunter knew one thing. He had to get Wayne Conrad out of here before things started blowing up around them. Because if he didn't, they could both be dead within a matter of minutes.

SIXTEEN

Chloe used her mom's phone and tried calling both her father and Hunter, which was probably not wise in this situation. But she had hoped one of them would pick up and tell her they were both fine.

Neither answered his phone. Then she heard her father's phone buzzing on his desk. He had it on silent.

She itched to run out into the frigid night, but she could see tiny snowflakes beginning to fall in the muted yellow of the security lights around the house.

"It's snowing, Mom," she called to Justine. "That can help slow the fire." But it would also make the night even colder and more dangerous.

"Oh, that's good at least," her mother called back. Chloe heard cups rattling and cabinet doors slamming. Her mom cooked when she was under stress. She'd probably have a gourmet breakfast waiting for all of them even though it was only half past midnight.

Chloe hurried into the kitchen. "I'm going to get us some heavy coats just in case we need them."

"And boots, too," Mom called. "Should I go with you back upstairs?"

"If you want."

Justine came hurrying behind her. "I don't want you out of my sight."

"I feel the same. Better to stick together for now."

Her mother gave her a concerned glance. "So you think this fire is deliberate?"

"Pretty sure. It can't be a coincidence."

They grabbed coats from her closet and her mother rushed to her room to change out of her robe. She threw on her own cozy boots over her slinky pajama bottoms.

They were on their way back down when Chloe remembered something. Hurrying to her room again, she found the gun she'd put in her purse at the cabin last night.

That seemed like a lifetime ago, but she'd been running on adrenaline for over twenty-four hours, and sooner or later, she was going to crash. Having a weapon would at least give her an edge if someone showed up unexpectedly. Chloe longed to stop and enjoy the snow, to be able to relax and be with her parents again.

But not right now.

Justine eyed the dainty pistol. "Good idea."

When they got back to the kitchen, the coffee was ready, the smell of the fresh brew filling the air.

"I heard the sirens," Chloe said. "Let's wait here for a little while longer. Once we see the fire department is here, we'll walk down and check on everyone."

"Okay." Her mother paced behind the long granite counter, her hair in silky tufts around her face. She finally turned to Chloe and said, "I still love him, you know."

"I know, Mom," Chloe replied. "I do, too."

"We'll figure this out together, Chloe," Justine said. "I didn't want to believe you, and I know your father didn't want to hear of it. It's too horrible to bear to think that someone killed our sweet, innocent Laura. And over what?"

Chloe didn't have the heart to tell her mother about what she'd found and about her suspicions regarding everyone around them. Besides, telling her mother everything was just too dangerous right now. Justine could keep a secret, but she'd spill any secret to protect the people she loved.

So she just said, "That's what I'm trying to find out. And I won't stop until I have the complete truth."

Hunter stumbled and hit hard against a metal table, a slash of pain throbbing across his cheek.

He rubbed his hand over his face and felt something wet and sticky. Blood.

"Over here."

He tried to follow Wayne Conrad's weakening voice. He was close now. "I'm coming. Hang on."

His eyes burned and itched and wet, hot sweat seeped from every pore and soaked his T-shirt, followed by a shivering cold that came rushing through the open doors. He heard the sirens and wondered if they'd ever get here.

Then he glanced up and saw a steel beam beginning to shake and tremble, a hungry heat leaping all around it. Hunter searched for the open doors. He'd never make it if that beam came loose.

"Lawson, help me, please!"

Hunter thought of how much he hated the man calling out to him. He thought this was the perfect retribution, to just let the old man suffer and die right here. No one would blame him. They'd never even know he'd heard Wayne Conrad begging for his help. He thought of his sweet, loving sister, Beth, a woman who wanted so much to make her marriage work that she'd lived with a cruel, uncaring alcoholic until he'd killed her. Then he thought of how this man, the one lying there in the fire, had manipulated the law and moved heaven and earth to keep his sorry son out of prison.

Until Hunter had decided to fight them.

"Lawson, help me!"

Hunter closed his eyes and coughed up smoke. He wasn't really a praying man, but he looked up toward where the Big Guy hung out. "Help me, God. Help me to do what I need to do."

With one last push of strength, Hunter got down on his hands and knees and crawled toward a corner. He saw a small window with a stray bit of light shining through.

That light guided him until he hit on a heavy figure huddled in a dark corner. Wayne Conrad.

But he was no longer conscious.

"Let's go down there."

Chloe saw the panic in her mother's dark eyes and felt the surge of that same panic beating against her heart. They'd waited long enough. Even though it had only been a few minutes, it seemed to drag like hours.

"Okay. Let's go. I have the gun if we run into anyone. I don't know what happened to the guards."

"Me, either," Justine said, her bravado returning now that they were going into action. "But they're both fired."

Clinging together in their big heavy coats and warm boots, they hurried down the slope of the yard and through the open gate to the outbuildings. The flames from the fire guided them, the smell of smoke and burned wood and melting metal bringing a sickening oily aroma wafting through the air.

"The fire truck is coming, Mother," Chloe said as they hurried toward the burning building.

"Where is Wayne?" Justine asked, her voice trembling. "What if—"

"I'm sure he's fine," Chloe said, her hand on her mother's arm. "We'll just have to make sure of that, right?"

"Right." Justine sniffed. "I'm a mess."

"You're strong and you're fine," Chloe said, her own body trembling from more than just the cold. Everything she'd been through in the last few days seemed to come crashing down with each groan of that angry fire. "It's understandable that you'd be upset. I'm upset, angry...and afraid."

Justine grabbed her with both hands. "Don't be afraid, darling. Remember when the angel came to Mary and told her 'Do not be afraid'?"

"Mom, this isn't—"

"It's the same," Justine said, gaining strength. "We can't be afraid. We don't have to be afraid. God is with us."

Chloe's eyes filled with tears. She'd always known her mother had a quiet faith that gave her a definite edge on life. But Justine had never before voiced it with such clarity. Laura had held that same kind of confident faith.

Chloe only wished her feelings were so strong. But she knew how to pray and she also knew that God was there even when her faith wavered.

"Thank you, Mom," she said, hugging Justine close. "I needed to hear that."

"I needed to say it," Justine replied, sniffing. "Now let's go find our men."

Our men?

Chloe's throat caught. Hunter. She could see it so clearly now. Part of her fear had been for her father's safety and part of it had been for her mother and herself. But the biggest part of what was driving her to run toward that fire was now front and center in her mind.

She was worried about Hunter. She needed him to be all right.

They made it within feet of the hissing, popping barn, the fire truck pulling up right behind them. Chloe pointed and shouted to the first man off the truck. "Two guards and my father and a friend are missing. We don't know if they're inside."

He nodded and relayed the urgency to the rest of the team as they went about accessing the situation.

Two firemen headed toward the open doors, their helmets and heavy uniforms protecting them as they went about their work. Chloe and Justine huddled together a few feet away, several live-in staff members joining them now that they'd been woken by the noise.

"Where is your father?" Justine kept whispering. "And Hunter? Where is Hunter?"

"I don't know."

Chloe was about to give up, her mind denying what could be the worst possible answer, when her mother glanced up and pointed a shaking finger toward the fire.

"Chloe, look."

Chloe whipped her head around and let out a gasp, her gaze caught on the huge open doors. There, silhouetted amid the ghastly flames of the fire leaping and hissing behind him, stood Hunter Lawson.

And he was carrying her father in his arms.

SEVENTEEN

Hunter fell to his knees and held tight to Wayne Conrad until the paramedics and firemen could help him get the unconscious man down onto the ground. They were both dirty and smudged with ashes and soot. The cut on Hunter's cheek burned with a searing pain that he'd managed to ignore up until now. Now his whole body seemed to scream in pain and his lungs felt as if they'd rusted and fallen into brittle pieces. He held back the memories of other such times when a buddy had carried another buddy out of a burning building, the screams of agony all around them like a constant echo that matched the rapid fire of machine guns and things exploding all around.

This wasn't that. Not by a long shot. He had to keep it together. For Chloe. For Laura. For Beth.

Once Chloe's father was safe with the first responders, Hunter collapsed back on his knees and held his head down while he took in air.

He wasn't sure if Wayne Conrad was still alive. Once Hunter had found him, he'd lifted him up and hurried to get outside. He hadn't had time to find a pulse. They'd made it out seconds before the big beam finally gave way and fell in a crashing shudder to the floor.

If Chloe's father was dead, that split second of indecision Hunter had felt there in the burning building would haunt him for the rest of his life. So he sat back on his heels and hoped Wayne would make it through. Not because he needed to be guilt free or because he cared all that much about Wayne Conrad, but because Chloe's heart would be broken yet again if her father died.

Then he felt a hand on his shoulder and looked up into eyes filled with tears and gratitude.

Her eyes.

"Thank you, Hunter," she said as she sank down beside him and hugged him close. "Thank you for saving my daddy."

She reached up and touched the jagged cut on his face and then she wiped away her tears and clung to Hunter until the EMTs came to give him oxygen and check his vitals and his wounds.

Two hours later, Wayne Conrad was in his bed being attended by his family doctor and a private nurse who'd been called in to sit with him through the night. Someone had knocked him to the ground and then kicked at his midsection. He had a cracked rib and he was suffering from the trauma of being caught in a burning building with toxic smoke boiling all around him. But with oxygen and a thorough check of his wounds, he'd been revived in a matter of minutes.

And then he'd insisted he was not going to the ER. He'd be just fine right here in his own home. After much arguing and a warning that his symptoms could get worse, the first responders had thrown up their hands and went about their business.

Soon, Justine was on the phone lining up his private physician and an around-the-clock nurse, and telling the EMTs she'd sign the proper paperwork because for privacy's sake her husband didn't want to go to the hospital.

Hunter had to agree with the woman.

Wayne Conrad had been attacked right before someone set his building on fire. He'd managed to tell Hunter and Chloe that much once he was revived. He'd also told them not to mention it to the locals. Even though they hadn't had a chance to discuss what had happened, Justine had whispered that they needed to keep him safe here at home. Hunter didn't bother pointing out the man had nearly been killed here in his highly secure compound.

Chloe's parents were now suspicious of everyone, same as Chloe and Hunter.

Conrad had told the sheriff that he'd gone out to the building when he saw the fire and he'd somehow fallen and gotten trapped. But since the fire department had found the body of one of his guards inside the burned-out hull of the building, Hunter and Chloe knew differently.

The other guard was still missing.

Hunter expected that sooner or later, the sheriff would find a way to finger him for setting the fire. That would work out conveniently for everyone. The man didn't seem to believe what Conrad had told him. He tried to get more out of the old man, but Justine took care of that by telling him to leave.

But Chloe knew the truth about Hunter's being here. And so did Wayne Conrad. He could only hope the old man would honor that truth once he was coherent enough to talk about what had happened.

Now Hunter sat with Chloe in the upstairs den.

Their den, as Justine had called it earlier. Hunter had showered, but he could still smell the chemical scent of electrical cords and burned wood and drywall all around him.

Justine had fed them dry toast and warm broth and then she'd insisted they both drink some awful-tasting herbal tea to help cleanse the toxins from their bodies.

Glad he'd survived *that*, Hunter listened to the quiet. Everyone had finally settled down around dawn.

Everyone except him. He'd tried to sleep and had dozed here and there, but he'd finally gotten up to come into the den to do some background work.

And he'd found her here.

Chloe lay curled on a cushiony couch with her eyes closed, a soft fleece blanket pulled over her. She'd obviously drifted off from pure exhaustion and Hunter had silently slid into a chair across from her and stayed quiet so he wouldn't wake her. She'd refused to go to bed, hoping to hear from her father again.

Conrad had been examined for smoke inhalation and given an antibiotic and some cortisone. After deciding he didn't have a concussion, the doctor had also prescribed a bronchodilator so Conrad could inhale the medicine on a regular basis for the next few hours. After a few coughing fits that only made his cracked rib hurt more, he seemed to be settling down, his nurse in a chair beside the bed.

The EMTs had stitched up Hunter's cut and given him an antibiotic for both the smoke inhalation and to ward off any infection. Since he'd recently had a tetanus shot, at least he'd convinced them he didn't need that.

Now a heavy fatigue settled over Hunter. He watched Chloe and wondered how he'd managed to save the man who'd made his life so miserable only a few short years ago.

He didn't regret saving Chloe's father.

He only regretted that he'd even considered *not* saving the man. Once he'd made the decision to help Conrad, that bit of light shining through the window had brought Hunter to his senses. He had to do the right thing.

His sister, Beth, had always taught him that.

"No matter what, Hunter, we always have to do the right thing. Sometimes, that's the hardest thing."

Beth had sacrificed to try and do right. She'd believed a marriage was for life, for eternity, and that you stuck it out through thick and thin, the way their parents had. But she'd paid for her loyalty with her life.

A twist of pain caught at Hunter and took away his breath.

The old bitterness pushed at him, trying to engulf him. He looked over at Chloe. Her blanket had slipped away. She wore some sort of soft shimmering tunic and matching pants. Her hair fell away from her face in shades of gold and brown. She shifted and let out a sigh.

Hunter's heart bumped an extra beat.

Now he fought against the pull of that sigh even more than he struggled to resist the barrage of old memories. He couldn't get involved with this woman. Too much water under the bridge. Too much pain built in a solid wall between them.

A golden curl fell over Chloe's right eye, slinking against her cheekbone like a finger motioning to him.

Hunter kneeled by the couch and gingerly touched his hand to the curl, his gaze moving over her face.

Chloe opened her eyes and saw him there. "Hunter," she said on a sweet, husky whisper that floated over him like a calming wind. "Hunter."

He moved to stand, but her hand touched on his stitches.

"Don't go."

She was so close. Too close. Her eyes widened as she came fully awake. When she tried to lift up he held her there. "Just rest. It's almost daytime, but you need to get some sleep."

She pushed at her hair and tugged at her pillows. "What about you?"

"I'll be fine."

"Who takes care of *you*, Hunter?"

That question floored him. He'd never considered it. "I take care of myself."

"Shouldn't be that way."

"Has to be that way."

She crooked a finger for him to come closer. Dangerous.

And yet, he couldn't stop the flood of emotions rushing over him like a dam breaking free. He leaned in. "What?"

"This." She lifted her head and kissed him on the cheek.

That should have been enough. But it wasn't. Not nearly.

Hunter lifted her up and sat down beside her and then he pulled her into his arms and kissed her. He savored the sweetness of this early-morning kiss and the strength he saw in her eyes each time she looked at him.

But he knew he'd have to let her go, sooner or later.

Their lives would always be intertwined, but he couldn't see them having a future together. He didn't do future. He lived for now and he took one step at a time, putting one foot in front of the other. He'd tried so hard not to look back, but now he could see that was all he'd been doing, really.

When he pulled away, Chloe's eye reflected all that he was thinking. Regret and longing merged with acceptance and disappointment.

"Don't say you're sorry," she whispered. "Don't say anything."

He smiled at that. "Don't you know that's how I speak? By saying nothing at all."

"Yes," she retorted. "You shout it loud and clear."

Then she snuggled into his arms and held him so close Hunter didn't dare breathe. But he didn't dare let go, either.

Chloe woke with a start and saw sunshine pouring through the big bay window across from the couch where she'd slept most of the night. Sitting up, she pushed at her hair and wondered where Hunter had gone.

Had he left just before the sun had come up to get away from her family and their problems? To get away from her and her feelings? To deny his own feelings?

The smell of coffee and the echo of voices caused her to drag herself out of the cocoon of covers surrounding her. Outside, a light dusting of snow covered the yard and the fields beyond.

But her gaze stopped on the burned-out shell of the building where her father had almost lost his life.

Hunter Lawson had rescued her father.

That heroic act sealed the deal in Chloe's mind. Laura must have known Hunter would find the truth. Chloe needed to admit to him that she'd seen his name on that paperwork and that that was probably the reason he was also a target. He wouldn't like it, but by now he'd surely have to understand it.

She washed her face and brushed her hair and then put on a touch of lipstick. When she walked into the kitchen, she found Hunter talking quietly with her mother.

"Good morning, darling," Justine said, rushing to hug Chloe. "How are you feeling?"

"Better," Chloe said, her gaze moving over Hunter.

"Hunter helped me with breakfast," Mom said as she handed Chloe some coffee. "He's actually a pretty good cook."

"Don't we have a cook?" Chloe asked to hide the myriad of feelings moving over her. They'd always had help, but Justine had loved to run the kitchen herself when she lived here.

"Yes, but I sent her home. What with everything going on here, we don't need any more people hurt…or worse." Mom poured herself another cup of coffee. "I've been fielding phone calls all day and I expect Gerald to show up any moment now. He sounded very concerned when I spoke to him earlier."

Hunter eyebrows lifted in a little twist at that remark. He sure didn't like her father's right-hand man. And Chloe had to admit she'd never felt completely comfortable around Gerald, either, but she tolerated him for her father's sake.

Chloe thought about the guard they'd found after the fire. She was sure the sheriff would be back to discuss that and the fact that the other guard was missing.

"Just don't tell the press anything," she said, cautioning her mother.

Justine lifted her hand in the air. "I know how to handle the press, darling."

"How is Daddy?" Chloe asked. "Can I go and see him?"

"He's sleeping," Mom replied. "But you can visit with him after you have something to eat."

"I'm not hungry."

"Hunter cooked French toast and bacon."

Chloe didn't want to be impolite. "I'll have a nibble."

She sank down across from Hunter, careful to divert her gaze away from him as much as possible. "Any word from the sheriff yet?"

"Not yet." He shot her mother a glance.

The room crackled with a tight tension.

"What are you two trying to hide?" Chloe asked, dread rising inside her chest.

Justine looked at Hunter, as if seeking his approval.

Hunter's slight nod indicated they'd been discussing something important.

"We got another message, honey," Mom said. "This time it came to me."

Chloe put a hand to her heart. "Oh, no. Mom, I'm so sorry. What did they say?"

Justine shook her head and put a hand to her mouth.

Hunter stared Chloe in the eye and spoke. "You've lost one daughter. Do you want to lose another?"

Chloe gasped and rushed to her mother. "Man or woman?"

"I think it was a woman," Justine said, tears in her eyes. "I can't bear that kind of threat. I won't put up with it."

"It won't happen, Mom. I promise."

"I can't trust your promise," Justine said. "I can't trust anything, not after your being shot at and our property being set on fire, your father almost dying. This is out of hand, Chloe. You need to drop this. I don't care what happened. I just want it to end."

"Even if she drops it now, it's not gonna end," Hunter said, his tone gentle but firm. "If we don't stop these people, none of you will ever be safe again."

Chloe could see it in his eyes. Hunter was in this for the duration. That was what made him so good at his job.

If they gave up now, he'd always be in danger, too.

"We can't give up," she said. "No matter what it takes."

Finally, she took a deep breath and said, "There's something I haven't told any of you. I think now is the best time to explain why I didn't mention it before."

Then she took a sip of her coffee and gave Hunter a grateful nod, the memory of their kiss last night fueling her need to find justice. And her need to find a way to keep Hunter in her life.

EIGHTEEN

Hunter grunted under his breath. This couldn't be good.

"Tell us," he said on a note of resolve while he kicked himself forty ways to tomorrow for ever thinking he could trust a Conrad.

Chloe's gaze moved from her mother back to him. "When I was going through the papers I found in Laura's apartment in Oklahoma City, I came across a lot of information."

Hunter shot her a warning glare. If she spilled what she'd found to her mother, Justine might feel obligated to blurt it all out to Wayne Conrad. But he was still high up on the suspect list in spite of what had happened last night.

Chloe's gaze held his. "But that was all scanned into a file I'd saved on my laptop, and since it got destroyed down in Florida, there's nothing I can do about that for now."

Hunter breathed a sigh of relief. Maybe she

didn't completely trust her mother, either. Or him, for that matter.

"But I found one thing that didn't seem to have anything to do with this, except now I'm thinking we might need to look into it, too."

"What?" both Justine and Hunter said at the same time.

Chloe looked directly into Hunter's eyes. "An article Laura tried to write about your parents."

"What?" Justine said again, giving Hunter a suspicious glance. "What do Bill and Mildred Lawson have to do with any of this?"

Hunter shook his head and tightened his lips. Was Chloe implying she'd located him not for his help but because she thought his parents were suspects? Had she been playing him all this time? "You said you found *my* name in her notes. You never mentioned my parents."

She studied her coffee cup. "I told you your name was written in the margin of some of the paperwork Laura had in a big box. *Hunter Lawson*, with a question mark beside it." Looking up at him, she said, "That's the truth. But later on, I found a pocket notebook. She used those when she was interviewing people. And, Hunter, she tried to interview your mother sometime last year. She went to Arkansas and tried to talk to her. Now I'm wondering if she *did* talk with your mother, but I never saw any article and her editor at the paper said she never wrote it. But she'd written your daddy's name on a page in big letters, too. And she'd circled it."

"Meaning what?" Justine asked, her attention focused on Hunter. The frown on her face showed just how much this new information was upsetting her.

Hunter felt the old rage boiling up. "If you'd mentioned that early on, I could have gone about this in a completely different way. You never once said my family was involved. How do I know you're telling me the truth now?"

Chloe pushed her hair off her face. "I wasn't sure I could count on you and honestly, I wasn't sure if this information had anything to do with my investigation. Laura interviewed a lot of oil patch workers. It was part of her job. Then everything happened and we were in this thing. I'm sorry. I should have explained this to you immediately, but I was afraid you'd tell me to get lost. Do you know anything about this? Why would Laura want to talk to your mom?"

"You're asking me?" Hunter said. He got up to pour himself some more coffee. "This is the first I've heard of this and I have no idea what it means. If I'd known anything about my mom being interviewed, I would have mentioned it right away. Which is what you should have done, too, by the way."

"Why would Laura go after your family?" Justine asked, her gaze on Hunter.

Hunter could think of several reasons a Conrad would go after a Lawson. Even Laura and Chloe. After all, he'd sent their stepbrother to prison. Could all this be aimed at luring him back to Oklahoma?

"I don't know," he admitted. "You people seem to have it in for us, for some reason."

"I think she wrote Hunter's name because she needed his help," Chloe said to her mother. "Or she'd decided that Hunter might have the answers she wanted. I don't know why she'd seek out your mother, Hunter. Unless it was to find you, of course."

Justine leaned back against a cabinet. "She could have thought he knew something about her findings. Laura was a stickler about verifying everything."

"It could be that, yes," Chloe replied. "Mom, stop staring at Hunter as if he's turned into a troll. We know we can trust him. He saved Dad's life."

"Where were you when the fire started?" Justine asked Hunter.

He should have known his welcome here wouldn't last long. They seemed determined to pin something on him, and this news only added to that notion.

"With your daughter," he said, leaving it at that.

That caused Chloe's mother to glare at him even more.

"We were in the upstairs den, Mom," Chloe said. "Talking. We both looked out the window and saw the fire."

Justine's expression changed and then she became flustered. "I'm sorry, Hunter. My nerves are on edge and…I don't understand what's going on. This latest is certainly strange." She let out a shuddering sigh. "But Chloe is probably right. If Laura wanted to seek you out to help her, maybe she wanted to warn you about something regarding her interview with your mother."

Hunter could accept that, but now he understood a lot more clearly why Chloe had shown up at his door. Seeing his name in those files and knowing Laura had discussed something with his mother must have triggered her need to find out what he might know. But Chloe had withheld this, the most important part of the puzzle. And yet she'd apparently led these people right to him.

"Why didn't you just ask me all this outright?"

"I wanted to tell you. I debated it in my mind over and over once I concluded that they might be after you, too."

He saw the trepidation in her eyes now. And the regret. "So when these people tracked you to Florida and then tried to shoot you, they probably were aiming for me, too, just as you suggested."

"Yes," Chloe said, staring directly into his eyes. "I should have told you that first night, but I was afraid you'd bolt. Or tell me to get lost. Or... come after my father."

"I probably would have done all those things," he admitted. "I tried to resist you. And yet here I am."

Justine's gaze moved between them. "I wonder why Laura wanted to see Mrs. Lawson."

Hunter shook his head, his gut burning. "Whatever it is, it can't come to any good."

Chloe's eyes met his. "I only found a date and a reminder, with a row of numbers. Laura jotted notes everywhere, and this one indicated she'd gone to Arkansas around this time last year, but your mother didn't want to talk to her. I filed that away, but I decided to find you."

"And you sure did," Hunter said, disappointment hitting him in his gut. "Found me and still kept me in the dark. I told you up front you needed to be completely honest with me."

"Are you angry?" she asked, their gazes holding while Justine took it all in.

"Shouldn't I be? I mean, I don't like being lied to or manipulated. And I sure don't like being shot at or accused of being a possible suspect. And now you tell me my family might somehow be a part of this? So you tell me, Chloe. How do you think I should feel?"

"I don't know," she said. "But you have to believe that I didn't withhold this information for spite or to manipulate you. I was afraid you'd refuse to help me. And then when it seemed so obvious that they were gunning for you, too, I panicked. I was worried that something would happen to you because of my actions."

"I can take care of myself."

"I know that now. I don't have any other secrets, Hunter."

Her mother actually snorted. "Hmm, I wonder about that."

But when Hunter looked over at Justine, her smile held a sweet sadness and an expression of motherly understanding. She gave him a forgiving nod and then hugged Chloe close.

"I need to go and check on your father," Justine said. "And I'm going to call Lorene Winston again. She's not answering her phone or returning my messages. I want to see how Bridget is doing, but your father warned me against going to the hospital."

"I appreciate that, Mom," Chloe said. "Let me know if you hear anything."

After her mother had discreetly left, Hunter stared over at Chloe. He was angry, but they had to keep at it, especially now. And she had to let him in. "Don't you trust me?"

"You should know I do."

"But you didn't tell me that my mama could be a part of this."

"I wasn't focused on your mother, Hunter. It was your name on a piece of paper," she said. "That started all this for me. I'd reached the end of the road and then I saw your name. And all the memories came flooding back—Tray and Beth and how my mother used to read the news coverage out loud to us like bedtime stories. When I found that little notebook and saw that Laura had possibly interviewed your mother, I saved it and moved on." She lifted her defiant chin and stared into his eyes. "My goal was to find you."

"But this was an important detail in the overall scheme of things, don't you think?"

"Yes, but you were the one detail I focused on. That one detail led me to you. So I can't be sorry I saw it or kept other things to myself."

He'd have to think about all this later. The distraction of her lips had him spinning into a dangerous daydream. So he fought at it by heading it off before it got worse.

"I shouldn't have kissed you last night," he said. "It was a moment of weakness."

He saw the hurt in her eyes before she blinked it away and lifted her shoulders in a shrug. "It's okay to be weak sometimes, Hunter. To show you're just as vulnerable as the next person."

He steeled himself against her words. He didn't like having his shell cracked open by that husky, gentle voice. "Only I'm not."

"Have it your way, then. I don't regret kissing you. And I don't regret *you* kissing me. In spite of everything, I kind of enjoyed it."

He remembered every second of that kiss, too. Her touch had been branded on his skin. But he didn't do this. He didn't get close to anyone. "You need to forget it."

"No, I'll remember it long after this is over. Long after you're still mad at me and fighting me."

Hunter would remember her, always. Because this would never be over. But he had to put these new, unsettling feelings out of his mind right now. The tentative trust they'd built had been torn in a fracture that only reinforced why he should keep his distance. Never trust a Conrad.

"Now that we have this new development, we need to regroup and get back on track."

"How do we do that?" Her expression held the question of what they should do about that kiss instead. And only made him want to try kissing her all over again. His mad was clashing with his attraction to her.

"We get back to business," he replied. "We'll talk to your father and ask him if he saw anyone in that building last night. He might have some answers for us on that. But we are not going to discuss my mother or my daddy with him, understand? I'll figure out what to do about my mother."

Wayne Conrad might be withholding details, too. And Hunter wouldn't put his ailing mother in danger, no matter what they found out.

"I haven't told him anything," Chloe reminded him. "And my mother won't tell him because she's guarding him like a hawk against any stress."

"Okay," Hunter said, trying to think ahead. "And we go and check on your safe-deposit box, just as we planned."

Chloe gave him a confident nod, but she looked away. "I can handle that. Back to business it is."

He wondered if he could handle any of this. Now he had the added task of finding out what, if anything, his mother might have told Laura Conrad. First, he had to call his mother and make sure she was okay. If she knew anything damaging, she could be in danger.

But after talking to her and then talking to his aunt, Hunter could tell they didn't have a clue what was going on. His mother didn't even remember Laura Conrad coming to see her. He asked his aunt about the security system he'd set up around the house they shared.

"We're fine, Hunter," she told him. "You do so much for both of us. We love you."

Why did he get the feeling his mother and his aunt were both holding back on him?

Between being highly attracted to a woman who was all wrong for him and being considered a suspect when he suspected everyone around him, Hunter felt a headache coming on.

He just ended the call with his mother when his phone rang and after hearing what Blain had to say, his headache increased to full-blown.

Chloe went into her parents' bedroom and found her mom sitting there holding her father's hand.

"How are you?" she asked, moving to kiss her father on his forehead.

"He needs to rest," Justine said before Wayne could speak.

"I'm fine," he interjected in a hoarse squeak before he went into a coughing spasm. "Just feel like I have a bad cold."

"You almost died, so you are not fine," Mom retorted. Then she insisted he drink more water. "I'm going to make you some lemon and honey tea."

"Take your time," Wayne shrilled after her. Then he turned to the hovering nurse. "I'd like to speak to my daughter in private. Please take a break."

The woman looked unsure, but she got up and left the room.

Once they were alone, Chloe sat down in the chair beside the bed and took her father's hand. "Daddy, why did you go out to that storage barn?"

Wayne looked her in the eye, his face sallow and pale, his eyes full of a wariness she'd never seen in him before. "I got a call."

Chloe's pulse accelerated. "What kind of call?"

"A woman. She said she had information regarding Laura's death. Told me to meet her out there."

"And you fell for that."

"She also told me she knew who was trying to kill you."

Chloe shook her head and rubbed his hand. "Why didn't you let Hunter and me know about this before you struck out on your own?"

Impatience colored Wayne's face a ruddy pink. "Because before I could alert y'all, I looked out there and saw the building was on fire. I rushed out and left my phone on my desk. When I got there, somebody hit me over the head and I fell. I thought I was a goner."

"Until I came along."

They both glanced up to find Hunter standing in the doorway.

"You heard all that?" Chloe asked, the sight of him there both a comfort and a confrontation.

"Yes."

He moved inside and stood at the foot of the bed. "It seems to me we could get more done if we all decided to come clean with each other. Details are kind of murky around here."

Chloe felt the sting of that suggestion. He certainly wasn't happy with her and he certainly didn't want to be here with her anymore. But he did want to end this.

Wayne's wary gaze moved between them. "Someone lured me out to that barn and tried to leave me for dead," he said. "That's what I know so far. The voice sounded familiar, but I can't place who it might have been."

"Do you think it was the woman who called you?" Hunter asked.

"I don't know," Wayne replied. "Could have been her."

Chloe glanced at Hunter. "Maybe we should—"

"I need to talk to you," Hunter said, obviously to keep her from blurting out everything they knew.

"I think I should hear what you have to say," Wayne said.

"You need to rest, Daddy," Chloe said. "I'll give you a full report as soon as we hear more."

"Have they found the missing guard?" Wayne asked, irritated.

"No." Chloe checked his blanket. "No word yet."

Hunter studied her father for a minute. "Did you see the person who struck you?"

Wayne shook his head. "No. It was dark and I was shoved from behind."

"Do you think it was the same person who called you?" Hunter asked.

"I told you I don't know. The phone call came from a woman, but I didn't see anyone when I got to the storage barn. Just felt a whopping blow that knocked the breath out of me and then smoke everywhere."

"Let him rest," Chloe said, the snap in her words causing Hunter to give her a harsh stare.

"I'll be waiting upstairs." Hunter pivoted and walked out of the room, his phone in his hand.

Chloe checked on her father again. "I have to go, Daddy."

"What's going on between you two?" Wayne asked, a quizzical expression on his face.

"Nothing that I can't deal with," Chloe retorted while she diverted her eyes.

"Are you sure about that?" her father asked, his question a mixture of concern and awe.

"No, but I will be soon."

"Be careful, Chloe," Wayne said. "Hunter's a loner and he has a lot of baggage."

"So do I," she retorted.

With that she hurried out of the room before her father saw the truth in her eyes.

She would never be able to handle anything Hunter Lawson did, because she was beginning to have feelings for the man.

But that could prove to be the worst mistake of her life.

Hunter didn't do happily-ever-after. He didn't even do maybe-we-could. He hated everything her family stood for, too. Another one of those important details she seemed to ignore.

He was only here to find out the truth, especially now that he thought his family was once again somehow tangled up with the Conrads. She'd dragged him into this thing and he'd see it through to the bitter end, no matter what.

That was what he was good at even if the man couldn't *see* the one glaring truth right in front of his eyes.

NINETEEN

"I got a call from Blain Kent," Hunter said once they were inside the little upstairs den. Flipping on the television, he turned up the talk show and then lowered his voice. "I'd called him last night to run down some information for me."

"What kind of information?" Chloe asked, her gaze doubtful.

A bright fire crackled in the fireplace. Outside, the fields were covered with a white dusting of snow. The roads were icy and treacherous, but Hunter wanted to be out there, riding away.

Far away.

Instead he turned to face Chloe. "Blain checked into the flight you took to get to Florida."

"Why? I used a private plane."

"Yes. But with the tail registration number, we can find out a lot of information on that plane. Blain called the airport where it landed and got the number. From there, he traced the plane back to the airport here."

"I used a small independent airport so no one would know anything," she said. "Did he find out something?"

"Yes, he did," Hunter replied. "He discovered who owns the plane you chartered."

"I know who owns it. OK Charters."

"And OK Charters is owned by... Wind Drift Pass Land Management Corporation."

Hunter watched as her face went pale. "What? That can't be right. I checked it out thoroughly because we'd never used that particular airport before. It's on the other side of Oklahoma City. Bridget helped me locate it."

Her eyes went wide with realization and shock. "Bridget booked the flight."

"Exactly," he said. "Bridget knows almost as much as you know about Laura's death. Bridget warned you against finding me. Bridget lured you to the cabin."

Chloe shook her head. "What are you saying, Hunter? That Bridget has something to do with this? We found her lying there half-dead."

"I know that," Hunter said. Unable to stop himself, he put his hands on Chloe's arms and turned her to face him. "But maybe she truly didn't notice the connection to Wind Drift Pass when she booked the flight. It would be hard for anyone to know that, based on the fairly generic name of OK Charters."

"So they tracked me to Florida, hoping to kill both of us and when we disappeared to come here, they came after Bridget?"

"Looks that way. Or…maybe Bridget knew exactly what she was doing and put you on that particular charter plane for a reason."

Chloe pulled away and stalked to the fireplace. "I can't believe that. She's been my best friend since grammar school."

"That doesn't mean a thing if big money's involved, darlin'."

"You think someone paid her off to make sure I used that charter service?"

"Another possibility. Or maybe she used that charter company because she knows a lot more about Wind Drift Pass than you do. Maybe she's in on something that she'd never told you about." He stared her down. "You know how people can withhold information such as this."

Anger colored her complexion a soft pink. "Yes, I know *I* messed up, but I don't think that's the case with Bridget. Hunter, you're just grasping at anything to figure this out or to punish me. If that's the case, someone could have killed me on the plane."

"That would have been too obvious. And we've established from the new information we now have that they seem to be targeting me, too. So they used you to get to me. Bridget is the link, Chloe."

"No, you're way off base."

"I have solid evidence that points to Bridget being either coerced into this or outright sending you to a certain death. The only reason they didn't crash that plane is that it would have been traced back to Wind Drift Pass. And we both know they don't want anyone to connect them to that."

She paced around, her hands on her hips. "I won't believe Bridget is involved in this. I can't. I'm going to my safe-deposit box to retrieve what few files I saved there. I'll find something in there to help me."

"To help *us*," Hunter said, not liking that dangerous stubbornness in her eyes. "I'm still on this case and now I have a vested interest in it."

"And I can still fire you," she retorted. "Especially if you keep accusing my best friend of being involved."

Hunter had to make her see reason. So he stepped in front of her and held her there. "Chloe, you have to listen to me or we're both doomed. Stop lying to me or I'll do what I have to, by myself."

Her eyes burned like a brush fire. "I'm listening but I just don't believe you. Not on this."

"Then I'll do my best to prove it, either way," he said. "And I'll go with you to the bank to get what you need from your box."

"I can do this alone," she said, still pouting, still stubborn.

Hunter let out a defeated sigh. "But you don't have to. Not anymore. That's the plan. That's why I'm here, so stop arguing with me."

"You make me a little crazy," she admitted. "All this is crazy." Her eyes went that soft alluring gold, apprehension shimmering through her gaze. "Is your mama okay?"

"Yes," he said, wishing he could stay mad. "For now. I had a security system installed at my aunt's house when she moved in, and they live in a gated retirement community. So I'm hoping nothing will come of this."

"I'm so sorry," Chloe said. "Please understand I've been so scared and…I'm so tired. I tried to tell you last night and then the fire took over and I just don't want anything to happen to anyone else, especially our families."

Hunter touched a hand to her cheek, the memory of holding her a strong tug on his senses. "We're in this together, okay?"

She stared up at him, the anxiety in her expression easing off. "Okay. Let me get my coat and purse. It'll be good to get out of here for a while."

Hunter nodded. "Just remember, I promised not to let you out of my sight. Even when you drive me nuts."

"I'll hold you to that, even when I'm angry with you."

"Isn't that pretty much all the time?"

She actually smiled at that and Hunter watched her walk toward her room, relief mixed with his own anxiety.

Blain had cautioned him to be careful on this. "If they're after both of you, there has to be some sort of connection. You need to focus on finding out what that is. And you might want to talk to your mom again and see what she'll tell you."

Hunter had become well aware of the situation.

Chloe had been a perfect lure to get to him.

And he had to wonder who would go to all that trouble.

No one that he knew of.

Except Chloe's father, of course.

Had this whole thing with the fire been yet another setup?

Chloe watched the snow-covered landscape moving by while Hunter pushed one of her father's SUVs to the limit. The roads were icy in spots, but I-40 was open all the way into Oklahoma City. Even the rows and rows of giant white windmills covering many of the fields seemed covered with a frozen sheen of ice. She just wanted to get to the safe-deposit box and get what she needed.

"So far, so good," Hunter said, glancing in the review mirror. "I don't think we're being followed."

"That's a relief," she said, her nerves spinning like those windmills that provided their own kind of energy and power to the people of Oklahoma. "I hope we can find something in those files I stashed that will help us."

They made it downtown, but the streets were deserted and the roads treacherous. Hunter seemed to know how to handle that. The man was a walking textbook of a highly trained warrior.

And...he knew how to kiss a woman.

That made Chloe's nerves shift from scared for her life to jittery with emotions. This wasn't supposed to happen. She'd never planned to actually have feelings for Hunter.

But she wouldn't deny her feelings. She just couldn't share them with him. He would leave then for sure. His whole persona shouted *no comment* and *no commitment*.

Chloe considered that a shield to protect him from all the pain he'd endured. He was a challenge, but she wasn't so sure she was up to that kind of emotional challenge.

They parked the navy blue SUV in the parking garage and then headed up the elevator to the bank.

"So, no one knows you have an account here?" Hunter asked as they rode the elevator.

"No. Not even Bridget." She shot him a look that dared him to comment on that. "I put these files here one day about a month ago when I went into a panic after seeing my daddy's name on that Wind Drift Pass contract."

"Do you have any other copies of the contract?"

"I had it scanned on my laptop and I put the original in the box here."

"So they took your laptop and destroyed it, but maybe they didn't find anything new?"

"I don't know what they found. I saved a lot of information. Some of Laura's original files must be missing. Maybe they took them when they raided her apartment."

"How'd you scan her files, then?"

"I only scanned the ones that offered me evidence."

He stopped when they reached the bank lobby. "Then where would she keep the rest of her files? Such as work files or business files? Sometimes you can find out a lot by looking at old phone bills or bank records and charge card activity."

"She stored a lot of her work files at the paper—the *Conrad Chronicle*. I had to beg to see them and I sure didn't tell her editor what I'd found. Eddie Bantam is one tough boss."

"We need to go there next," Hunter said. "First, let's check out what we have here."

They went through the process of signing in and Chloe showed the bank manager her picture ID. Then they were guided into the area where the safe-deposit boxes were kept and Chloe and the bank manager both inserted the necessary keys. Once they had the box, the bank manager stepped away but stayed in the vault. Chloe opened it and stared inside.

Only to find it completely empty.

"It's gone," she said, her heart exploding. "The contract and the other papers, all gone."

"Someone seems to know your every move," Hunter said. He turned to the confused manager. "Who else has been in here?"

"I don't know," the jittery little man said. "You saw our procedure. We verify with signatures and locks and even video sensors." He looked at Chloe. "Miss Conrad, only you and anyone you registered as your agent of record can access this box."

"Did you name someone as a corenter?" Hunter asked Chloe.

She closed her eyes and nodded. "Yes. Bridget."

"I thought you said no one knew about this," Hunter said.

"I meant no one out there—I'm so used to Bridget being my shadow that I didn't include her in that category. But I didn't tell her why I needed this box."

"Well, that doesn't matter now," Hunter said. "It backs up my theory that Bridget might not be so trustworthy."

Chloe felt sick to her stomach. She turned to the manager. "Has my assistant Bridget Winston been in here recently?"

"I'd have to check the records and the surveillance video," the man said. "I'm not always here, but no one comes into this vault alone. I can ask the other bank executives."

"Please do," Chloe said. "Those papers were important."

"I'm so sorry," the man said. "I can assure you we'll do everything in our power to find out what happened."

"That won't bring back those files," Chloe said. Then she stared down into the empty box, the weight of trying to find the truth almost too much to bear. Lowering her voice, she said to Hunter, "We need to go to the paper and I think we need to check Laura's apartment again, too."

Without her laptop or the contents of this box, it would be hard to prove anything that she'd found or seen. No one would believe her. Had Bridget gone behind her back to erase everything she'd found?

After they'd filled out a report on the missing

contents and the bank manager assured them he'd found out what had happened, Hunter guided her out of the building. "Someone really doesn't want this to leak out," he said. "They've obviously destroyed your laptop and any remaining evidence that they found."

He glanced back to where the flustered manager stood talking to a staff member. "They claim they don't know what happened, but we can view the video and find out. Somebody got to your box. And they probably dressed up to look like you in order to do it."

"And you think Bridget was that person?"

"Well, who else could it be? Think about it, Chloe. If she's the corenter, she wouldn't have to fake her way in here. She could come right in and take whatever she wanted."

"I don't know. What if someone pretended to be Bridget? That could be possible, since she rarely comes in. Her being a corenter was just a formality. Someone could have dressed up like her, put on a red wig and forged her signature."

"Possible, but a stretch," Hunter replied. "We'll have to wait and see what the other employees remember and see what the surveillance video shows."

"Another roadblock," Chloe said. "I never considered that Bridget might be capable of anything like this. Things got hectic last week when

I made the decision to find you, so there's no telling what she knows. But she might not ever wake up to tell me."

"We're getting closer with each step," Hunter said, still stunned that she *had* found him and that she'd decided to locate him based on his name written in the margins of her sister's files. "And we'll muscle the bank to let us see any video footage that might show who came here. That could give us a strong piece of evidence."

"Thank you, Hunter," she said, her heart settling back down. "You truly are the only person I can trust. I should have seen that from the beginning."

He gave her a resigned glance. "This thing is big, Chloe. Maybe too big for the two of us. But we're not gonna give up until we've retraced your steps and Laura's every move, too. Sooner or later, these people will have to reveal themselves."

Chloe admired his determination. She just wondered how much it could wind up costing them to retrace all those steps.

TWENTY

She was quiet.

Too quiet.

But then, the streets were quiet and still. The whole downtown area and the surrounding countryside seemed posed for something to happen. Hunter realized why he loved Florida so much. No skyscrapers where he lived now. No one lurking about either. Well, at least not until Chloe had come to town.

They'd been by the newspaper office, but Laura's files, notes and papers weren't there anymore. It was as if everything about her had been wiped away.

"I sent what we found to your mother, Chloe," the desk clerk told them. "I'm so sorry."

"Is Eddie here?" Chloe asked, glancing around.

The young man looked uncomfortable. "No. He…transferred away after Laura died. We haven't heard from him in months."

Another person gone missing. Another part of the puzzle.

Hunter checked the streets and then he checked on Chloe. And wondered what Justine might have done with Laura's belongings. "I know it's hard to accept that Bridget might be involved, but—"

"She's not. I'm sure there's an explanation for all this. Just like there has to be an explanation for Laura wanting to talk to your mother."

"Touché," Hunter replied.

He saw this in black and white. From what he saw, Bridget had been involved from the beginning. Bridget was high on his suspect list. But he still had to figure out how his family played into this.

He tried again. "But—"

"I don't want to talk about it."

He reached over, trying to take her hand. He'd never been one for fancy words or grand gestures, but he wanted her to know he understood her disappointment and frustration. "Chloe…"

She ignored him. Turned toward the passenger-side door. Then she mumbled, "I've messed up so badly. I wish I could make it all right again."

Hunter glanced at the road ahead and then back to her.

The vehicle was suddenly slammed from behind with such a jarring force Chloe bounced and went forward, hitting her head on the windshield.

"Chloe!"

Hunter looked behind them. The downtown area of Oklahoma City was nearly deserted because of the snowstorm. A huge souped-up pickup truck slowed and then geared up again. It was coming for more.

Chloe moaned and touched her head.

Hunter saw blood on her fingers. "Are you all right?"

"Yes. Just go."

He sped up, but the icy roads caused him to spin out. Regaining control, he looked in the rearview mirror. The exit to the interstate was ahead and uphill. He decided to take a sharp turn to the right.

"I'm going to try and lose 'em. Hold on tight."

Chloe nodded and pulled a tissue out of her purse. "Haven't we been here before?"

"Yes. And we'll be here again, too."

After that, the chase was on. No shooting yet but just a determined pursuer who relentlessly tried to run them off the road. But Hunter swerved and dodged, ran through a few traffic lights and managed to find a back road out of town.

"We'll be okay," he said to Chloe. "If we find a turn, we'll lose them."

"Do you think Bridget sent them from her hospital bed?" Chloe asked in a terse shout.

"No, but I think someone is pulling all the strings...with Bridget and with the people on my bumper."

They took another hit. The whole SUV shuddered in protest and the crunch of metal echoed over the deserted road.

Hunter looked ahead and saw a curve. He had to make it around that curve or he might not get away from the people chasing them. Once he lost these idiots, he'd find a way back to the interstate road.

He touched his foot to the gas pedal, careful not to over accelerate on the icy roads. The snow was coming down again and up ahead the woods surrounding the road had become dense with almost barren trees and thick patches of bramble.

They'd almost made the curve when the truck following them made one more pounding attempt. The heavy front bumper and thick grill looked like a laughing face as the driver shoved close and held the gas pedal to the floor.

Hunter gripped the steering wheel of the skidding SUV, but in a matter of seconds, the vehicle slid and started spinning like a top. Black ice.

The last thing Hunter saw before the SUV spun off into the woods was the other truck careening off into a shallow ditch on the other side of the winding road.

He heard Chloe scream and then he heard an explosion.

And then his world went black.

Chloe felt the chill of wet, cold air on her face. Her whole body hurt with a burning heat that only warred with the frigid wind. She blinked, opened her eyes and saw Hunter passed out across from her, air bags floating around both of them like grotesque giant marshmallows.

"Hunter?"

He didn't move.

Swallowing back pain and panic, Chloe tried to unhook her seat belt, but the airbag kept pushing at her. Her chest hurt from the force of the airbag exploding and her head hurt from the bump against the roof of the truck. Twice.

"Hunter? Answer me! Please!"

Chloe smelled an acrid smoke that only brought back memories of last night and the fire. She glanced back and saw the other vehicle turned over back in the distance, billowing smoke moving up through the snow.

That only reminded her of their night on the Bay Road back in Millbrook Lake. Those two men had never been found. Could that have been them again?

The heavy smell of gasoline caused her to go into motion. With a grunt and a jerk on the seat belt, she gritted her teeth against the agony that screamed down her arm, but she managed to break free and fall out of the battered door on her side. Then she stumbled down into the mud and dirt, her boots sinking. Gripping onto the twisted bumper, Chloe lifted herself up and managed to make her way around to Hunter.

"I'm coming," she said into the cracked window. "Hold on, Hunter."

The door wouldn't open.

Searching her jacket pocket for her gloves, Chloe felt the tube of lipstick she'd found on the closet floor of the cabin.

Laura's lipstick. Her sister had been a girly-girl. Always primping and playing with color. A shard of longing shot through Chloe and tears brimmed in her eyes.

"Help me, Lord. Help me. Don't let Hunter die. I can't take someone else I care about dying too soon. I don't know what to do anymore."

Closing her eyes against the dizziness, Chloe wished Laura was still alive. But that couldn't happen. They'd see each other again one day, but for now she only had this little tube of lipstick to cling to. But that gave her the encouragement she needed. Laura would tell her to put on some color and find a way to help her friend.

Chloe checked the vehicle and saw gasoline dripping from the busted gas tank. One spark and this whole vehicle would explode in the same way as the one following them. She prayed the wet snow would take care of that problem.

But she had to find a way to get to Hunter.

And she needed to find Hunter's phone so she could call for help. First things first. She had to get Hunter out of the truck.

So she grabbed the door handle with both hands and tugged with all her might to get it open. Her fingers grew stiff and numb with cold, but she kept pushing and pulling and then she heard a click. With one more burst of energy, she tugged on the door.

The door opened and knocked her back, causing her to stumble and fall hard to the ground. Lying there, she heard the crunch of something moving through the forest.

Someone.

Chloe pushed herself up, pain radiating all over her body. She hobbled to the SUV and shoved at the airbag until she had Hunter out from under it. With another grunt she managed to pull him part of the way off the seat.

"Hunter, you have to wake up. They're coming for us."

With cold, shaky hands, she felt his pulse. Weak. But he was still alive. Then she checked his face. A few lacerations but nothing major. After pushing her hands through his hair, she felt a large knot right over his left temple.

No blood, but it had to have been a hard knock. He must have hit it on the roof or the headrest when they bounced so hard against the forest floor. Then she saw a spot of blood near his stomach.

A gunshot wound. They must have shot at them the last time the truck rammed their vehicle.

The footsteps kept coming, slowly but surely. Someone had survived the other crash.

Chloe held Hunter's head in her hands. "Hunter, I need you to wake up."

He moaned and blinked. "What? Where are we?"

"The woods. We crashed. You're hurt."

He moaned and went slack again.

Frantic, Chloe glanced around for some kind of weapon and spotted her purse lying on the floor near Hunter's feet. Her gun was inside that purse. Twisting her arm around his boots, she managed to drag the big purse up and over until she could reach in and grab the gun.

The footsteps had stopped. Where had they gone?

Hoping whoever it was had passed out, she searched Hunter's pockets and found his phone. Armed with that and the pistol, she went to work on getting Hunter down on the ground. Dragging and pulling, she huffed and used all her strength to get him out feetfirst.

Hunter's feet hit the dirt, but he started slipping. Chloe caught him in her arms and shoved him against the vehicle, his phone in one pocket and her gun in the other.

Then she heard the footsteps crunching again, a slow steady gait hitting against the shards of ice and snow. The smell of gas and oil grew stronger, burning at her cold nose.

"Hunter," she whispered in desperation, "we have to get out of here."

He moaned again and touched a hand to her hair. "I'll…figure…out a…way."

But he was in no shape to figure anything out. It would be up to her to keep them alive.

With another grunt, she shoved Hunter down into the snow and went down beside him, the open door their only protection. Desperate, she grabbed some snow and rubbed it over Hunter's face.

The cold, wet mush caused him to wake up and open his eyes.

He took one look at Chloe and saw her holding the gun and tried to lift up.

"Stay," she said on a soft whisper in his ear. "Somebody's nearby."

Hunter pulled her toward him and lifted his body in front of her. "Give me the gun."

"I've got it," Chloe said, shaking her head. "You're too woozy."

"I'll be okay. Chloe, give me the gun."

Chloe was about to argue with him when a movement caught her eye. Looking beyond Hunter, she went on autopilot and lifted the gun into the air. She trained it on the man approaching them with a silenced gun, finally getting a good look at him. Her hands began to shake and she hesitated. But before she could recover and pull the trigger, she felt a strong, firm hand over hers.

The man stalking toward them was bloody and battered, but he held up the weapon and aimed. Bullets pinged and popped all around them while she held Hunter close and tried to shield him. Chloe heard a hiss nearby.

"We've got this," Hunter said on a rush of breath as he took her into his arms.

And then together, Chloe and Hunter shot back, his hand over hers as he pulled the trigger and fired.

The woods went silent again.

"I had it," Chloe managed to whisper, the aftereffects of the whole thing causing her hands to shake as tremors of shock and cold moved down her body. She stared at the spot where the man had fallen and saw a deep red stain in the snow.

Hunter's eyes held her. "I know you did. I wanted to help."

Still reeling, she touched her hands to his face. "We have to get *you* some help. You've been shot." She pulled his phone out of her pocket, that hissing sound reminding her of the danger of staying here. "And we have to get away from this truck before it explodes."

He glanced down at the blood on his shirt. "You have my phone?"

"Yes. I don't have one of my own now, remember?"

She held it up and hit 911. Nothing. "No signal."

"Figures."

"Can you walk?" she asked Hunter. It was getting late in the day and she didn't want to spend the night in these woods.

"I'll walk. Don't worry."

Chloe moved up against the door and offered him her hand.

"No. I might pull you back down." His eyes burned a deep green. Even now he was flirting?

Chloe hid the smile that seemed to want to burst through her fear and pain. She couldn't afford to smile right now.

She stood, watching as he slid up and tried to

stand. After a wobbly start, he grabbed the door frame and laid his head against it.

Chloe leaned in and held him. "Hunter, we need to find you a doctor."

"You, too," he responded.

Then he tugged her against him. "I'm sorry I didn't take care of you."

Chloe's eyes filled with tears again. "Shut up. That's all you've done for the past week."

"Our first date."

"Yeah, well, maybe our second one won't involve chases and fires and guns."

"Will we have a second date?"

"I haven't decided," she said, sniffing back the emotions threatening to take over. "Let's get out of these woods and we'll talk."

Hunter did one of his infamous grunts and lifted himself up, determination sheening in the sweat on his beat-up face. "Okay. Let's walk out to the road and we'll decide from there."

Chloe nodded, too tired and wrecked to speak.

Because here in the midst of crashed cars and stalkers and guns blasting, she'd just realized she had fallen in love with Hunter Lawson.

TWENTY-ONE

Hunter went into full survival mode, ignoring the pain in his head and the throbbing in his side. The bullet had gone through; that much he had figured out when he probed around and felt the exit hole in his back.

"I'll be all right," he told Chloe over and over. He used snow to clean the wound and he stanched the bleeding with by applying pressure. Both the cold snow and the pressure shocked him awake. Chloe found a scarf when she grabbed her purse from the truck. Then she dragged him away from the truck and found a fallen log for him to sit on while she wrapped his wound and tied it tight with the wispy piece of fabric. She'd just finished when the SUV exploded and burst into flames, the heat warming them where they sat several yards away.

No help there.

Now they were trekking alone on a deserted, frozen road and the sun was going down while the snow increased with every step they took. The coming night promised to be brutally cold. Right now the wind laughed and hissed around them with a glee that made Hunter grit his teeth.

"Chloe, we have to find shelter."

"I know," she responded, her voice full of shivers.

She wore a wool hat and a lightweight wool coat over her sweater and jeans. At least she had on suede boots with sheepskin linings. But if they didn't find shelter, they wouldn't survive out here with the temperatures dropping.

He kept checking the road for dirt lanes or driveways. To distract her from interrogating him over and over about his burning wound, he finally asked the one question that had been on his mind since they shot that man. "Why did you hesitate?"

She looked up, her hat hiding her eyes. "What are you talking about? When?"

"You know when. You had a perfect shot back there, but you hesitated. And I don't believe it was out of fear or doubt."

She didn't speak at first. Then finally she said, "I knew that man, Hunter. He's the missing guard from my daddy's house."

Hunter stopped on the road to stare over at her. "Are you sure? I didn't get a good look at him the other night or today. He was always wearing a hat or looking down."

"Yes," she said, lowering her head. "But I'd know him anywhere. He's been employed with my family since I was a teenager. He's driven me to school, taken me to the mall, sat with me at the dentist office. You name it, Martin Rhimes has done it."

"I don't remember him," Hunter said, wishing his head wasn't so jumbled. "I should have taken his ID."

"It doesn't matter," she retorted. "I can ID him. If we ever make it home."

Hunter planned on getting her home, and soon. "Tell me about him."

"He made his way up the ranks and hit the top after you'd moved on," she said. "He's been one of my daddy's bodyguards since I was a teenager. I can't believe he'd do this."

Hunter saw the anguish in her eyes. "And recently? Has he been around *you* recently?"

"He drove me to the airport the other night. For my flight to Florida."

"Why him?"

She inhaled a breath. "Bridget sent him. Said he was the only driver available." Putting a hand to her mouth, she added, "Oh, no. This can't be happening. Bridget's name keeps coming up in spite of all my denials. Hunter, this is bad. Worse than I ever imagined."

Hunter had to agree with that. "So either he or Bridget could easily have downloaded that spy app on your phone. And he probably sent the hit men to Florida."

"Yes. And he's probably been shadowing me for months now. I'm sure my daddy hired him to watch out for me after Laura died."

"He could have killed you at any time, but he's obviously hoping to find what they need first. He had to have been a good shot and yet he missed when he fired at us today."

She moved her head in a slow nod. "There was something in his eyes. Regret, remorse. A plea. I froze when I realized it was him."

Hunter pivoted her around. "So you couldn't shoot him in spite of realizing he was betraying you."

"No. I looked into his eyes and I just couldn't pull the trigger. I can't believe…we killed him. I wish I could have asked him why. Maybe he would have told us the truth."

"He tried to kill us, Chloe," Hunter said, the harsh facts as cold as the brutal wind. "He made his choice. He decided to die rather than rat out the real culprits."

"This will break my daddy's heart."

"I think his heart is already broken."

"Hunter…"

"Let's get you somewhere warm and safe, okay?"

He couldn't do this. He wouldn't cave right here on this desolate, cold road. And he wouldn't let her freeze to death tonight. He kept her moving, forcing her to put one foot in front of the other for the next hour. He let her talk, too. She told him about Laura and how they used to play together near the oil fields, or ride horses in the big pasture. Her sister had been her best friend and her champion.

"Her one flaw was that she was too open and trusting. She believed in the best in people, didn't look for the worst."

Just like his sister, Beth.

The old pain stabbed at him and he wanted to hate Chloe Conrad. But he couldn't hate her. He had never hated her. He only wanted to save her. And find the people who were hounding both of them.

When they reached an incline, Chloe stumbled and fell. She wasn't going to last much longer. She was coming down from all the adrenaline and the chaos. She'd crash soon.

Hunter lifted her by the arm and put his hand over her shoulder. "Just a little while longer, okay? Gotta keep moving."

"Tired." But she kept walking. She was a trouper.

Hunter closed his eyes and said a prayer. He and God hadn't been on very good terms lately, but because of Beth's abiding faith in him and Him, Hunter kept the Big Man on speed dial.

"I need You now," he whispered. "Don't let me fail on this mission. I failed many times over and killed in the name of war and I've done horrible things, but don't let me fail tonight, Lord." He kept Chloe moving. "She deserves your grace even if I don't."

The night howled with that wind that never died. The snow drifted in soft, lacy flakes so beautiful they tricked the mind into believing they were a safe, soft blanket.

Hunter kept moving, practically dragging Chloe. She was quiet, didn't fuss at him or try to resist him. He wanted her to argue with him and fight him and question him.

He didn't know how much time went by, but a half-moon rose high in the sky, guiding him, encouraging him. But he knew about the dark side of that moon.

Chloe moaned and collapsed against him. "So tired. Need to rest."

"I know, baby, I know."

Hunter lifted her up into his arms, his wound tearing and screaming against the effort. But he carried her, praying, hoping, and willing himself to keep moving. And he thought about all the times he'd carried a fallen warrior in this same way, dragging, coaxing and finally picking up an unresponsive buddy to carry him home. He'd cared deeply for all of them and wished each time that he'd been the one to fall.

Now his heart hurt for this brave, confused woman in his arms. Now he had a new fight to finish.

He's almost given up hope when he looked up and saw a mailbox up ahead, its reflector light shining in the woods. Hunter ignored the tears freezing against his face and started toward that beacon, his steps hurried now.

He kissed Chloe on the forehead. "Look. I think we've found a place. I've found a place."

She didn't respond.

Warmth.

Chloe felt warmth surrounding her. She sighed in her sleep and snuggled against the security of a broad chest, the crackle of the fire making her so sleepy. She should wake up, but she couldn't. This felt so good. So right. Maybe she'd never wake up. Maybe she'd stay in this safe, secure dream forever.

Then she heard a distinct male grunt and opened her eyes.

Hunter.

They were on an old worn couch that sat in

front of a roaring fire. A cabin or hunting camp maybe? Rustic and plain, old and run-down, creaky and dark.

Perfect.

She looked up at Hunter. His eyes held hers in a warmth that rivaled the fire.

"Hello," he said without smiling.

"Hi." She sat up but stayed near him. "How are you?"

"I'll live."

He felt warm. Too warm.

"Hunter, I think you have a fever."

"I said I'll live."

She loved his grumpiness. She loved his softness.

She loved him. "Where are we?"

"Oh, just a little resort in the middle of Oklahoma."

"I don't suppose this resort has room service?"

"Nope. I found some Vienna sausage and what could have been potatoes at one time. The sausage is probably safe, but the potatoes, not so much."

She grimaced and sat up. "Water?"

"Yes. Bottled and a spigot out on the back porch. I recommend the spigot. It's icy cold."

Her throat was parched. "I'll get us some."

"No, let me." He tried to get up and fell back.

"You need to stay there," she said, noticing the pallor on his face.

She slipped off the couch and found a clean cup and then spotted a pitcher full of water that he must have drawn from the spigot earlier.

"Here," she said, sitting down next to him. "You first."

She knew he wouldn't drink until after she did, so she took a small sip and then another greedy one. "There. Now drink."

His smile was overshadowed by his beard stubble and the dark circles underneath his eyes.

"Did you sleep?" she asked, pushing at her hair.

"Some."

"You need to rest. I'll be fine."

"I'd rather watch you."

"Aren't you tired of me by now?"

He sat back, his dark hair fanning out on the cushiony couch. "You're kind of growing on me."

Chloe walked around, stretching her sore body. "I guess I don't have a concussion," she said, touching on her head. The wound was clean now.

"I checked you over. You're tough."

"Let me check you over, then."

"I checked me, too," he said. He shifted and made a face. "Sore and bruised but I've been through worse."

She didn't try to hide her concern. "Did you doctor your wound?"

"I cleaned it with water and some soap I found on the counter." At her look of horror, he said, "It was antiseptic soap and still good. I checked the date."

That gave her some relief. But his fever worried her.

"We need to get out of here. Have you tried your phone?"

"No service and little battery."

"What now, Hunter?"

He patted the sofa. "We wait for daylight. Just a couple of hours."

Chloe sat down beside him, suddenly tired again. "What a night."

"What a week."

She bobbed her head. "I was so afraid I'd lost you yesterday."

"I'm hard to kill."

She stared at him for a minute and then reached up to swipe at his inky bangs. "Will you do something for me?"

"Depends."

"Tell me about Millbrook Lake."

He smiled at that. "Well, the sun comes up early there. I like to run around the lake early in the morning just so I can see that sunrise. Sometimes I run all the way to where the river meets the bay and stand there, watching the sun coming up. It's a view I never get tired of."

"That sounds so pretty."

"It's a good place to live. The houses around the lake are all historic and Victorian. My friend Alec has the biggest one because he has a lot of money. But…he doesn't let that go to his head. He's a good man. I have good friends there."

He told her about Marla's wonderful cupcakes and other confections and Blain's need to protect everyone. He talked about Aunt Hattie, who sounded like everyone's favorite loving aunt. He told her how he'd met Blain right here in Oklahoma and how they'd stayed friends. He told her about Preacher and how he worked to be the spiritual compass for all of them.

"I have to get back to be in his wedding," he said, his voice low and gravelly. "I promised him."

"When is the wedding?"

"The Saturday after Thanksgiving."

"Next weekend?"

He squinted as if he'd just realized how soon that was. "Yes."

"Then you'll be there, regardless."

"I want you to be there with me."

"What?"

"I can bring a date."

"But do you often do that? Bring a date."

He reached out his hand to her. "Never before. Usually, I don't even bring myself."

Chloe took that moment to let go of all the

emotions she'd been holding so tight. "Hunter... what's happening with us?"

"I don't know."

She didn't want to cry, but the tears seemed to seep out of every pore of her body. "I wish—"

"Don't wish, sweetheart. Don't think about it."

"What can I do to stop this? What can I do to make life normal again so I can attend that wedding with you?"

He gazed at her with eyes that told her what he couldn't say. Misty-green eyes that held dark secrets.

"We'll find them, Chloe. I know we will."

"I killed a man today, Hunter."

She fell against him and started crying. She didn't want to have a meltdown, but she was tired and sleep-deprived and her heart hurt for what he'd lost and for how much she wished her sister hadn't been murdered. That God could bring them together like this—that was the only saving grace in this whole thing.

That realization gave Chloe the strength she needed to keep moving. She glanced up into Hunter's eyes. "I don't want to give up. I can't give up. Hunter, all this brought me to you and I have to wonder if Laura knew I'd see your name there in her files. I have to wonder if she orchestrated this whole thing, just in case something happened to her." Chloe sat up, wiping at her eyes. "She always loved a good puzzle or a scavenger hunt. She was good at winning games and figuring out all the dynamics in a situation. I think she knew we'd find each other."

She grabbed at his jacket. "I think God knew we'd find each other."

Hunter's eyes held hers. He didn't speak, but the expression on his face told her everything. He still held her hand and now he tugged her into his arms and held her there, kissing the top of her head, kissing her lips. Holding her tight.

Chloe searched her jacket pockets for a tissue. She didn't like to cry. It hurt too much. She just wanted the truth—

Her hand touched Laura's lipstick again. She sat up and stared over at Hunter, clutching the lipstick tube in her fingers. "Hunter, I think I might know where Laura hid the rest of the information."

Hunter stared at the lipstick. "In a tube of lipstick?"

"No, in a tube of lipstick that's really a flash drive."

She tugged on the top of the slender silver tube. They both stared at what they were seeing.

"A flash drive inside a lipstick tube," Hunter said, hugging her close again. "Who would have thought?"

"No one. Laura's that smart. She must have

dropped it in that closet on purpose because she knew we both kept clothes in there."

"And that has to be the key to all this."

"Now I'm really going to cry," she said. "We can't look at this till we make it home but if this contains what we think it does then this is almost over. Finally."

Hunter smiled over at her while she recapped the flash drive back inside the sleek tube. "Your sister *was* smart."

She couldn't stop the tears. "Yes, but I'm not so smart. I've been carrying this around for days, right under our noses."

"Cry, Chloe. Cry all you want. I promise I'm not going anywhere until you're safe."

"Crying is a sign of weakness," she said, ashamed of herself.

Hunter kissed her on the cheek. "No, darlin', it's a sign of something that transcends weakness. It shows you have a heart. Remember what you told me? It's okay to be weak sometimes."

Chloe touched at his hair. "Have you ever bawled like a baby?"

"Yes," he said, the admission shattering her to the core.

"Then you *do* have a heart, too, Hunter. You need to remember that."

"I found my heart again," he said, his eyes on her.

Then he wrapped his arms around her, warming her. "Why don't I tell you some more about Millbrook Lake? In the spring, it's especially—"

The door burst open, sending a blast of frigid wind and icy snow all over the small cabin. Someone shoved Chloe to the dirty floor and threw a dark bag over her head.

TWENTY-TWO

Hunter felt a starburst inside his brain and then saw Chloe being hauled away with a bag over her head.

"Chloe?"

Her scream was the last thing he heard before he blacked out.

When he woke up, he heard another familiar sound—the wind howling in an angry, brutal scream that echoed off this cold room. His head hammered in protest each time he blinked, but he wanted to see where they'd brought him. And he prayed Chloe was somewhere nearby.

"She's not here."

Hunter blinked, tried to move. His hands were tied behind the chair. Looked like he was about to be interrogated.

He looked at the man he'd hated for a long time now and wondered why he hadn't confronted him from the beginning. "What did you do with her?"

"She's in capable hands, so relax. They'll be

here soon. She's receiving a tour of our lovely facilities right now."

"If you hurt her, I will kill you," Hunter said with such assurance the other man backed up and flinched. But only for a second.

Gerald Howard moved in close and stared down at Hunter with a dark gleam in his eyes. "I have to say, you are one hard man to get rid of, Lawson. You might have beat Wayne Conrad at his own game before, but you won't be so lucky this time." He slapped at Hunter's face. "You've got me to deal with now."

"I can deal with you easily," Hunter said, a fierce hatred giving him strength.

"You should have stayed in the Sunshine State."

"I left here," Hunter reminded him. "I planned to never come back. You didn't have to get rid of me. I was gone long before I crossed the state line."

"But she just had to find you. Such a noble attempt at honoring her sister's misguided attempts to seek the truth."

Hunter worked at the ropes holding his hands behind him. "And what is the truth, Howard?"

"Don't you know yet?" Gerald said, his hand on the arm of the old office chair where Hunter sat. "You're such a smart guy. Everyone says you can crack any case. Has this one got you stumped?"

"I'm beginning to see the big picture," Hunter

said while he took in his surroundings. Looked like an old construction trailer or guard shack. Dirty and dingy and smelly. Cold and full of boxes and a beat-up desk and filing cabinet. They had to be on an oil field somewhere. Or a vast piece of land.

"You're the mastermind behind all this and I'm pretty sure the old man doesn't have a clue that you've been forging documents in his name and doing something highly illegal at Wind Drift Pass." He leaned up, his hands working against the old, dry ropes. "I'm guessing you sent Sonny down to fetch Chloe home and you set that fire the other night, but why? Did you want to kill your boss?"

Howard's eyebrows lifted. "That? A miscalculation. A distraction so we could search that fortress. But my man panicked when he heard the sirens. He didn't get through the whole house."

"Your man? Must be the one we left back on the road. He's dead now just like poor Sonny."

Gerald Howard's black eyes flickered with anger. "Laura Conrad should have stuck to writing about puppies and nursing home birthdays. But those sisters are too nosy for their own good. And so are you."

"How did Laura stumble into all this?" Hunter asked, his every pulse beat focused on knocking this man off his high horse and finding Chloe.

Howard stood and tugged his wool coat collar over his ears. "Funny thing, that. Laura did a series of interviews on some oil field widows. You know, the sob story kind that makes everyone hate the work we do."

"A human interest story," Hunter said on a low growl. "Tugs at the heartstrings."

"Yeah, a little too much." Howard leaned down again, this time both hands on Hunter's chair. His gray-blond stiff hair stood out around his face like a brittle patch of bramble. "One of the women she interviewed was your mother."

Hunter tried to come out of the chair. Howard had just verified his worst nightmare. But Chloe had said Laura never finished the interview. "If you hurt my mother—"

"Relax. She's fine. Still in that retirement home in Arkansas last I checked."

"Just the fact that you've been spying on my mama is reason enough for me to beat you to a pulp," Hunter said. "She's safe now and happy with family nearby. You stay out of Arkansas." He took a breath. "But wait, I won't have to worry about that. You'll be behind bars for fraud and a whole host of other illegal acts soon enough. If I don't kill you first."

"I'm not the one with my hands tied behind my back, son," Howard said, standing again. "Now, where was I? Oh, yes, your mother, the dear woman, told Laura about a small parcel of land your daddy owned and how someone from Conrad Oil had shafted it and several other tracts right out from under him."

"What are you talking about?" Hunter asked, shock knocking him back. "My daddy didn't have that kind of money."

Howard chuckled. "That's where you're wrong. Your daddy took a lot of bribes and worked some odd jobs for the Conrads—well, he thought he was working for the Conrads. I paid his salary."

"That's a lie. You're lying to cover your own hide. What are you hiding on this land, Howard? Illegal dumping, drilling without permits, using Conrad's equipment illegally? What?"

"Your daddy knew all about that kind of thing. Too bad you can't ask him. Too bad I'll have to tell you the truth about how your sister really died."

Beth? Hunter's anger gave him a rush of adrenaline. "What are you talking about?"

"You'll never know."

Hunter stood up, bringing the chair with him. He didn't break loose, but he managed to knock Gerald Howard down. While the older man tried to get up, Hunter kicked at him with all his might and finally broke free of the flimsy ropes.

Dizzy with pain and his bullet wound piercing like a knife against his side, Hunter rammed his body into Howard's and sent him flying. The other man fell against an open metal shelf full of tools and hit his head. He went down in a slump against the wall and wailed a low moan.

Hunter grabbed him by the lapels and jerked him up. "Tell me what's going on, Howard. Or I'll finish it here and now."

Then he heard the rattling door of the metal building swing open. The wind and snow warred against each other while a chilling blast of winter air rushed through the flimsy building. Shoving Gerald against the wall with an elbow to the man's throat, Hunter gritted his teeth and watched the door.

Chloe was standing there with Lorene Winston. And Lorene held a gun to Chloe's back.

Chloe saw Hunter and let out a relieved gasp.

Earlier, she sat shivering in a cold corner where a lone lamp burned a feeble halo over her, the darkness beyond full of shadows and shapes that she'd finally saw as huge dump trucks. She prayed for Hunter. She prayed for her family. And she hoped that when they killed her it would be quick and over with soon.

She remembered Hunter and how he'd described Millbrook Lake. She thought about her time there. The bright pumpkins and colorful mums on the big rambling porches. The manicured yards full of palm trees and mushrooming live oaks. The breeze off the lake and the sound of gulls cawing overhead. Graceful egrets and elegant blue herons moving in the shallows. Sailboats floating by and little boys fishing off the marina pier.

A place to call home. A beautiful place because she'd found her heart there at a dive called the Hog Wash Rib Joint.

She wanted to go back to that place and never leave. She wanted to curl up beside Hunter on the couch inside that cute little house where he'd tried to make a home. She wanted to show him that his heart was bigger than Oklahoma and that together, they could both heal.

But the woman standing over her now with a gun aimed at her had other ideas. Lorene Winston had been in on things from the beginning. Apparently, Gerald and Lorene had teamed up to hide the truth from everyone. But Laura had stumbled onto that truth and now so had Chloe and Hunter. Bridget had become suspicious and she'd almost lost her life, too.

She looked at Hunter now, her heart breaking from what Lorene had told her. "Hunter?"

"Are you all right?" he asked, moving toward her.

"Stop right there," Lorene said. Then she heard Gerald's painful moan. Waving the gun at Hunter, she shoved Chloe toward him. "Help him or I'll shoot her."

Hunter's gaze flickered over Chloe, but he turned to Gerald Howard. He pulled Howard forward, but Lorene pressed the gun into Chloe's ribs. "Let him go."

Hunter shoved Gerald down. "He's all yours."

Lorene tried to help Gerald up, but he pushed her away. "It's all right, darling. Now we can sit down and have a civilized chat."

"There is nothing to chat about," Lorene shouted. Her crazed stare moved between Chloe and Hunter. "I'll never forgive you for what you did to Bridget," she said on a hiss of anger.

Chloe shook her head. "It seems to me you're the one who harmed your daughter. And my sister, too. Why did you do it, Lorene? Why would you put Bridget through this and have Laura killed?"

"I told you," Lorene shouted, spit coming out of her red lips. "If you hadn't forced Bridget to help—"

"And I told you, Bridget and I didn't know you and Gerald were behind this but he must have had Bridget put me on that plane. You're cruel and…evil. Evil. That's the only word for someone who'd have her own daughter brutalized."

Lorene slapped her, causing blood to pool on

her lip. Chloe gritted her teeth and stared up at the woman who'd been ranting at her for hours.

Hunter lunged forward, getting in Lorene's face. "If you lay a hand on her again, I will take both of you out. I want the truth. All of it."

Gerald slowly stood and held a hand on Lorene's arm. "Let them sit. We'll end this soon enough." He shrugged, his smile full of indulgence. "My sweetheart is anxious to leave the country."

"You don't get it, do you?" Lorene said, motioning them to two rickety folding chairs. "It's really your fault, Mr. Lawson. You started this horrible situation. You put the wrong man in prison. Gerald, tell him the truth about how his precious sister died in that car crash."

Hunter went still, his whole body turning to stone. Chloe inched her chair closer to his and reached for his hand. But he pushed her away. He couldn't bear to be touched right now.

Gerald Howard's grin was full of malice and spite. "I made a fortune with this land and it all started when your daddy bought a couple of acres here. He wanted to settle down and farm, but he didn't have the backbone to do what needed to be done. He couldn't walk away from the oil patch. And then he did something that changed his life forever."

"What?" Hunter asked, anger pouring over him. "What are you talking about?"

Gerald Howard glared down at him, glee filling his mad eyes. "He went after Tray Conrad on a rainy spring night. Tray beat your sister up and forced her into the car with him. Tray was drunk out of his mind, but Beth was driving the car that night."

Chloe gasped, her gaze meeting Hunter's.

Hunter's heart hammered a raging pain. He stood and yanked Howard up. "What are you saying?"

"Your daddy took his shotgun and followed them. Only he didn't know Beth was driving and with the storm brewing, he couldn't see. He shot into the car and...well, you know the rest. The car crashed and Beth died. You put away Tray, but your daddy is the one who killed your sister."

"No!" Hunter shoved Howard hard against the wall, every pore in his body rejecting what he'd just heard. He ignored Lorene's shouts and Chloe's screams. "You're lying. I know you're lying. Tray was driving the car. It came out in the trial."

"Tray was so drunk he couldn't remember, so he thought he was driving. But I'm telling the truth because I was his lawyer. I fueled Tray's grief and let him drink all he wanted. Convinced him he did it, but I promised I'd make sure he didn't go to jail. Because I knew the truth and I knew how to use that truth."

In a fatherly fashion, he touched a hand to Hunter's arm. "Son, your daddy came to me, crying his eyes out, and confessed. He needed my help. Everyone always needs my help."

Chloe's soft cries echoed over the room. "Hunter…"

Hunter hated the pity in her voice. Hated this shack and the world outside.

Howard's voice went low and Hunter saw the evil in his eyes. "And that's when I knew I had him. For life. Your daddy became one of the best midnight haulers in the business. Because he didn't want your mama and you to know what he'd done."

"No, no." Hunter shoved him away and bit back tears and bile, his breath coming in shards. He tried to blink away the weakness surrounding him. "No."

Chloe grabbed him and held him up. Hunter fought against that soft shield, but he didn't push her away. He couldn't push her away even when he wanted to hate her, too.

"Yes," Lorene shouted. "Yes. That's the big secret Laura Conrad wanted to bring to light. She was trying to clear her stepbrother's good name. But she messed where she shouldn't have. You all did. Even my precious Bridget."

Hunter let out a primal scream and slammed his fist into Gerald Howard's face and heard bone crunching. The older man stumbled, but Hunter caught him. "You blackmailed my old man into doing your dirty work, didn't you?"

Gerald Howard stared into his eyes and nodded. "Yes, son, I did. But you won't live to tell that story." He nodded toward Lorene. "Time to use that fancy gun, Annie Oakley."

Chloe thought she was going to be sick, but she took one look at Hunter's ashen face and found the courage she needed to survive. While Lorene gloated and held the gun between her and Hunter, Chloe watched and waited.

Lorene turned to her. "Which one should I shoot first, honey? Which one should suffer the most?"

Chloe gave Hunter one last glance and hoped she could convey all that she felt in that one split second. "Take Hunter first. He's suffered enough."

Hunter gave her a shocked stare and then he laughed. "She's right, you know. I don't mind dying at all. Do it, lady!" He turned and jumped toward Lorene, causing the woman to step back.

Right into the booted foot Chloe lifted to kick her.

They went down in a pile of sweaters and hair.

Lorene screamed and held the gun up, but Chloe grabbed her hand and yanked it back, trying with all her might to force Lorene to drop the gun. Lorene screamed and grunted, her feet kicking, her free hand pushing and shoving at Chloe.

Chloe managed to roll over and pin the other woman to the floor. With a scream and a final push, she held Lorene's arm in a twisted angle until the other woman moaned and finally let go of the gun. Then Chloe slid to the side and grabbed the gun before Hunter could get to it.

But Lorene came up and tried to grab it, too. The gun went off, the echo jarring the decrepit shack.

Lorene Winston's body slumped over and went still.

Chloe fell to the floor and closed her eyes.

Hunter watched in horror and held Gerald Howard in a death grip until he heard the shot. Screaming, calling out to Chloe, he knocked Gerald Howard down and rushed toward the two women.

"Chloe?" He called her name over and over, fear and anger forcing him to keep moving in spite of his spinning head and pain-seared body. "Chloe, answer me!"

He reached her and lifted her up. She opened her eyes, tears streaming down her face.

Hunter held her, stroking her hair. "Are you all right?"

She bobbed her head. "I think I just killed Lorene Winston."

Police cars and sheriff's department SUVs lined the muddy dirt road leading up to the building. Hunter sat with Chloe on the back of an ambulance, watching as investigators gathered evidence and the EMTs took care of Gerald Howard and Lorene Winston. Gerald had a bump to the head and Lorene had a gunshot wound in her right shoulder, but she would live.

Hopefully to serve a long time in prison.

Hunter ignored the fever sending chills up and down his spine and glanced toward the hulking warehouse not far from the old shack. A warehouse full of dump trucks.

They'd finally found Wind Drift Pass.

It was a virtual pond of toxic sludge and oil patch mud. Nasty mud full of vile chemicals that would seep through the ground and pollute the drinking water and possibly the land itself for miles and miles. Gerald Howard had bought it up acre by acre and hired desperate men like Hunter's brokenhearted daddy to haul the illegal waste and dump it here. And he'd done it all in the name of Conrad Oil. Wayne Conrad had a lot of explaining to do, but Hunter knew the old man hadn't been involved in this. Knew it in his burning gut.

"Mr. Lawson, you really need to get to the ER."

Hunter pushed the anxious paramedic away and closed his eyes to the horror of this night. How could he ever get past this? How could he ever get past what he'd done to find justice for Beth? It didn't matter that Tray Conrad had been a sorry, mean drunk and a cruel, abusive husband. He hadn't been driving the car—

"Is it really over?" Chloe asked, her voice low and hoarse.

It would never be over.

"I think so," Hunter finally replied. "Did you give them the flash drive?"

"Not yet," Chloe said. "I still have trust issues. I want to see what's on it first."

He'd like to see that, too. But the thought made him shake all over again.

Chloe snuggled into the blanket the EMTs had covered her with. "Hunter, do you believe what they told us?"

He turned to her, wishing he could wipe it from his memory. "I don't want to." She reached for him again, but he shook his head. "I'm sorry. I don't know how to come back from this, Chloe." Throwing off the blanket smothering him, he said, "I should never have come back here."

She pushed on, fear in her words. "They could have made that up. It might not be true, Hunter. Please don't do this to yourself."

Hunter couldn't speak. His skin burned hot against the frigid air. His head hurt with a constant throbbing brutality, and the hole in his stomach scorched him with each breath he took. He finally got up and walked away. He'd done what he'd set out to do. He'd exposed the people who'd killed Laura and tried to kill Chloe. But his sense of justice and the truth had been shattered into a million pieces.

He didn't know how to recover. He didn't know what to do now. He thought of Chloe and how she had changed him in ways he wasn't yet ready to admit. He couldn't do this. So he called Alec Caldwell.

"I need one more favor," he said. "I need to get out of Oklahoma."

Then he turned and passed out cold.

TWENTY-THREE

The next afternoon, Chloe stood on a cold tarmac and watched as a stretcher carrying Hunter Lawson boarded the private plane Alec Caldwell had sent to bring him home.

Alec stood with her, the wind moaning and crying all around them, the white scar along one side of his face furrowed with worry. "I've never seen him this way. I guess he'll tell me what happened when he's good and ready."

Tears pricked at Chloe's eyes. Her father had heard the news late last night and had promptly gone into his office and shut the door. He'd be okay, but he'd called Chloe in and told her he knew nothing about all this and that somehow he'd work to make it right. Her mother had cried all night and hugged her over and over. Bridget had come out of her coma and didn't remember much about the night they'd tried to kill her.

They had yet to tell her that her mother would probably be spending a long time in prison, right along with Gerald Howard. They'd underestimated Laura and Chloe Conrad.

Chloe had seen the contents of the flash drive. Laura had meticulously spelled it all out in chronological order after she interviewed Hunter's mother. She'd pieced it all together and she'd included pictures of the trucks, license plates and even names, including Bill Lawson's name. The number Chloe had found on that tiny notebook page matched the name of the folder stored on the flash drive. And Bridget's mom had been the one to go to Chloe's safe-deposit box. The bank had verified that. She'd posed as Bridget.

"I didn't get to see him last night," she told Alec now. "He needed to rest and… I didn't know how to tell him how sorry I am. He made it clear that he was done." Wiping her eyes, she looked at Alec. "Take care of him."

"Always," Alec said, understanding in his steady gaze. "He won't want to be taken care of, but we'll do it anyway."

She stared at the sleek plane. "I can't tell him goodbye."

Alec took her hand in his. "I have a feeling you'll see him again, Chloe."

Then he smiled and turned to board the plane.

Hunter woke to the sound of jet engines revving. Squinting, he saw a murky Alec leaning too close. And behind him, Blain and Rory looking morose and solemn. "What? Another bachelor party?"

"You're going home," Alec said, his tone firm. "Your wound got infected and you had a slight concussion, hardheaded man that you are. Just rest."

But Hunter couldn't rest. Grabbing Alec's coat sleeve, he said, "Detour. Hot Springs, Arkansas."

Alec's frown changed to a resolved understanding. "Detour it is. I'll inform the pilot."

One week later

Flowers filled the entire altar. Flowers of every color and shape and smell. Soft candles burned bright yellow-tipped flames on either side of the altar. Soft music flowed out over the crowd gathered here in the tiny Millbrook Lake Church to celebrate the marriage of Rory Sanderson and Vanessa Donovan.

Hunter stood with Alec and Blain next to Rory, his mind numb with grief and pain. His body was healing, but his heart was still torn and scarred. He missed Chloe with each breath.

But he couldn't face her. His mother had verified the truth that had torn their world apart.

"Your daddy died of a broken heart and I couldn't bring myself to tell you why. I was a coward and I hated myself for it. I'm so sorry, son. I let you fight them all because I blamed Tray, no matter how Beth died. He forced her into that car and he's the one who deserved to die. You and me, we've suffered enough. We have to forgive all of them. And… Hunter, please forgive yourself. Your sister loved you so much."

Not so easy.

He'd stayed out at the AWOL house once they made it back to Florida. Blain, Alec and Rory sat with him one long night and forced him to tell the whole story. Torture, but a healing kind of pain that had left him drained and exhausted.

"I think your mom is right," Rory said. "Forgive. Not for them. But for you."

Blain rubbed his five o'clock shadow. "You should call Chloe. She can take you, bro. I think she's pretty tough."

Hunter shook his head. "I sat right here with y'all a few months ago and said I'd never fall for anyone. I can't face her. It's over."

Alec thumped him on the head. "I saw her when they loaded you onto the plane. It ain't over. She loves you."

He hadn't had the guts to tell his friends he loved her, too. That would be his secret.

Now he only wanted this sweet showing of love

and commitment to be over so he could go back to being himself. But he'd never be the same.

Marla brought Roxie to see him one day and after heating him some soup and shoving two big chocolate cupcakes at him, she left the little mutt for the night.

"Roxie misses you," she said.

He'd cried that night. And told the little dog snuggling in his lap, "If you squeak this to anyone, I'll never give you treats again."

Roxie had licked his face and settled back onto his stomach, her trusting eyes absolving him.

Now the wedding song started and Hunter stood stoic and solemn in his fancy threads and tried not to think about the woman he'd left in Oklahoma. She was supposed to be here with him. He wanted her here with him.

But that was just a part of something he had to let go.

So he watched a preacher friend of Rory's perform the marriage ceremony and he stood for pictures and then followed everyone over to the house that Vanessa and Rory would live in—Vanessa's inherited house across the street from the church—and tried to enjoy the reception set up in the big back garden. More candles and pretty music, a fire pit to keep the chill away, people laughing and happy, Roxie roaming around.

Roxie barking as a beautiful woman walked down the steps from the big back porch. Roxie turning to him with a hopeful doggy smile as if the little imp knew and approved.

Chloe.

Chloe in a flowing red dress and silky floral shawl with her golden curls caught up in a glistening clip. Chloe with hope in her eyes and tears misting on her face.

He glanced around, his heart bursting wide-open, and then he gave in to a piercing need and walked toward her and held out his hand. "You came."

She looked him over in a slow burn. "You left."

He nodded, held her hand. "I had to sort through some things. I didn't think—"

"I quit my job."

He'd get the details later, but…now…now he only wanted to dance with the woman he loved. "I can't dance, but—"

"I'll teach you."

He took her into his arms and held her there. "That means you'll have to stay here with me for a long, long time."

"You're a slow learner?"

"Yes. Very slow." Then he asked, "What about your father and me—"

"He expects you at dinner next Thanksgiving." She looked around and smiled. He didn't dare glance back, but he was pretty sure his buddies and their women were gleefully watching this whole thing play out.

"I like this place," she said, her voice husky and low. "I think I might just stay for a long, long time. That is if—"

"I want you here," he finished.

And then he kissed her and felt the rip in his heart coming back together, solid and safe and sure.

"Tell me," she whispered. "Hunter?"

"I love you," he said, his nose in her hair. "I love you."

She lifted her head and stared into his eyes. "I love you, too. Laura used to say 'Love never fails.' We owe it to her and Beth to believe that."

They stood that way for a few more precious minutes. Then she said, "I'm starving. Can you feed me?"

"Always," he said. Then he turned and grinned at his friends and the beautiful women who also believed that love would never fail.

They all applauded and whooped and did high fives and then everything became a beautiful blur of pure joy.

Roxie barked her way between them, so Hunter scooped the little poodle into his arms and laughed. She licked his face and glanced back at his friends with that knowing little doggie grin.

Someone was watching him.

And this time, Hunter knew exactly who that someone was.

* * * * *

Dear Reader,

Hunter Lawson came into my head one day when my husband and I were visiting a friend in Oklahoma City at a biker bar after I'd spoken to a local writers' group. I saw a lone man sitting out on the deck, looking away from the crowd inside. Then I saw another biker ride up on a fancy motorcycle and yes, he had a little white poodle riding shotgun with him. I imagined the story about the man sitting there alone. Then I decided he needed that little poodle to cheer him up. That's how Hunter Lawson became real to me.

Normally, I don't hang out in biker bars, but out of that scene came four books about Millbrook Lake, Florida (a town I based on several small Florida towns). The original plots changed a bit with editorial direction, but the characters that popped into my head stayed with me. I hope you enjoy Hunter's redemptive story. I wanted this story to show that even when we do something for all the right reasons, things can still turn out in a tragic way. But God will see us through with love and mercy. God's word is all about forgiveness and unconditional grace.

I hope to add one more book to my Millbrook series. I keep wondering whatever happened to

Santo Alvanetti (the brother of Rikki in *Her Holiday Protector*). Hmmm.

Until next time, may the angels watch over you. Always.

Lenora Worth

LARGER-PRINT BOOKS!

GET 2 FREE LARGER-PRINT NOVELS PLUS 2 FREE MYSTERY GIFTS

Love Inspired®

Larger-print novels are now available...

REQUEST YOUR FREE BOOKS!
2 FREE WHOLESOME ROMANCE NOVELS IN LARGER PRINT
PLUS 2
FREE
MYSTERY GIFTS

☀☀☀☀☀☀☀☀☀☀☀☀☀☀☀☀☀☀☀☀

HEARTWARMING™

☀☀☀☀☀☀☀☀☀☀☀☀☀☀☀☀☀☀☀☀☀☀

Wholesome, tender romances

YES! Please send me 2 FREE Harlequin® Heartwarming Larger-Print novels and my 2 FREE mystery gifts (gifts worth about $10). After receiving them, if I don't wish to receive any more books, I can return the shipping statement marked "cancel." If I don't cancel, I will receive 4 brand-new larger-print novels every month and be billed just $5.24 per book in the U.S. or $5.99 per book in Canada. That's a savings of at least 19% off the cover price. It's quite a bargain! Shipping and handling is just 50¢ per book in the U.S. and 75¢ per book in Canada.* I understand that accepting the 2 free books and gifts places me under no obligation to buy anything. I can always return a shipment and cancel at any time. Even if I never buy another book, the two free books and gifts are mine to keep forever.

161/361 IDN GHX2

Name _____ (PLEASE PRINT)

Address _____ Apt. #

City _____ State/Prov. _____ Zip/Postal Code

Signature (if under 18, a parent or guardian must sign)

Mail to the **Reader Service:**
IN U.S.A.: P.O. Box 1867, Buffalo, NY 14240-1867
IN CANADA: P.O. Box 609, Fort Erie, Ontario L2A 5X3

* Terms and prices subject to change without notice. Prices do not include applicable taxes. Sales tax applicable in N.Y. Canadian residents will be charged applicable taxes. Offer not valid in Quebec. This offer is limited to one order per household. Not valid for current subscribers to Harlequin Heartwarming larger-print books. All orders subject to credit approval. Credit or debit balances in a customer's account(s) may be offset by any other outstanding balance owed by or to the customer. Please allow 4 to 6 weeks for delivery. Offer available while quantities last.

Your Privacy—The Reader Service is committed to protecting your privacy. Our Privacy Policy is available online at www.ReaderService.com or upon request from the Reader Service.

We make a portion of our mailing list available to reputable third parties that offer products we believe may interest you. If you prefer that we not exchange your name with third parties, or if you wish to clarify or modify your communication preferences, please visit us at www.ReaderService.com/consumerschoice or write to us at Reader Service Preference Service, P.O. Box 9062, Buffalo, NY 14240-9062. Include your complete name and address.

WESTERN WP PROMISES

YES! Please send me **The Western Promises Collection** in Larger Print. This collection begins with 3 FREE books and 2 FREE gifts (gifts valued at approx. $14.00 retail) in the first shipment, along with the other first 4 books from the collection! If I do not cancel, I will receive 8 monthly shipments until I have the entire 51-book Western Promises collection. I will receive 2 or 3 FREE books in each shipment and I will pay just $4.99 US/ $5.89 CDN for each of the other four books in each shipment, plus $2.99 for shipping and handling per shipment. *If I decide to keep the entire collection, I'll have paid for only 32 books, because 19 books are FREE! I understand that accepting the 3 free books and gifts places me under no obligation to buy anything. I can always return a shipment and cancel at any time. My free books and gifts are mine to keep no matter what I decide.

272 HCN 3070 472 HCN 3070

Name	(PLEASE PRINT)

Address	Apt. #

City	State/Prov.	Zip/Postal Code

Signature (if under 18, a parent or guardian must sign)

Mail to the **Reader Service:**
IN U.S.A.: P.O. Box 1867, Buffalo, NY 14240-1867
IN CANADA: P.O. Box 609, Fort Erie, Ontario L2A 5X3

* Terms and prices subject to change without notice. Prices do not include applicable taxes. Sales tax applicable in N.Y. Canadian residents will be charged applicable taxes. This offer is limited to one order per household. All orders subject to approval. Credit or debit balances in a customer's account(s) may be offset by any other outstanding balance owed by or to the customer. Please allow 4 to 6 weeks for delivery. Offer available while quantities last. Offer not available to Quebec residents.

READERSERVICE.COM

Manage your account online!
- Review your order history
- Manage your payments
- Update your address

> *We've designed the*
> *Reader Service website*
> *just for you.*

Enjoy all the features!
- Discover new series available to you, and read excerpts from any series.
- Respond to mailings and special monthly offers.
- Connect with favorite authors at the blog.
- Browse the Bonus Bucks catalog and online-only exculsives.
- Share your feedback.

Visit us at:
ReaderService.com